## About the Author

I am Māori and Pacific Island Mixed Heritage residing in Perth, Western Australia. My iwi is Ngāi Tahu and Te Āti Awa.

# People of the Clouds

Willa Cadman

---

People of the Clouds

Vanguard Press

**VANGUARD PAPERBACK**

© Copyright 2024
**Willa Cadman**

The right of Willa Cadman to be identified as author of
this work has been asserted by her in accordance with the
Copyright, Designs and Patents Act 1988.

**All Rights Reserved**

No reproduction, copy or transmission of this publication
may be made without written permission.
No paragraph of this publication may be reproduced,
copied or transmitted save with the written permission of the
publisher, or in accordance with the provisions
of the Copyright Act 1956 (as amended).

Any person who commits any unauthorised act in relation to
this publication may be liable to criminal
prosecution and civil claims for damages.

A CIP catalogue record for this title is
available from the British Library.

ISBN 978 1 83794 153 7

This is a work of fiction. Names, characters, businesses, places, events and
incidents are either the product of the author's imagination or used in a
fictitious manner. Any resemblance to actual persons, living or dead, or actual
events is purely coincidental.

*Vanguard Press is an imprint of*
*Pegasus Elliot Mackenzie Publishers Ltd.*
www.pegasuspublishers.com

First Published in 2024

**Vanguard Press**
**Sheraton House Castle Park**
**Cambridge England**

Printed & Bound in Great Britain

This book is enriched by the knowledge of Ngāi (Kāi) Tahu family members whose contributions are instrumental to its value and worth. I have taken some creative license with their initial storytelling to give a possible context for mythological evolution. But, without their contributions, The Emerald Water Tribe would be a shallow pool rather than a robust running river filled with treasures. I believe there is always some truth behind a story and the greatest thing to creative writing is the ability to bend stories to fit a narrative that gives a source of reality. Therefore, Uncle Edward Ellison, Paulette Tamati-Eliffe, Tumai Cassidy, Maringi Osborne from Kāi Tahu Iwi, Otakou, Te Waipounamu, the Dansey Road Conservation group, Rotorua, Bay of Plenty New Zealand, I thank you for the gift of sharing your knowledge aiding the understanding of our culture to all people across the world that show an interest.

# Chapter 1

# The Hunt and the Fist

The night before her excursion, she had tried to position herself closest to the door for an early escape; deliberately hiding in the furthest corner of the big house near the doorway.

The corner was dark. A cold breeze blew in uneven gusts through the small cracks, making it unpleasant and difficult to find sleep. Not a favoured place to sleep by most people. But the location, close to the door, suited her purposes well. She pulled her blanket tighter around herself, tucking the edges under her legs to block out the cold air that seeped in. Her subtle movements caught the attention of the tall thickset muscular sentry on duty who peered intensely into the darkness, pointing the tip of his spear menacingly in her direction.

"Move in, Aõ," he grunted at her.

"Why you so near the door? Did Ranger have too much pork tonight and is farting?" the guard joked, chuckling to himself at his lame wit.

"Move, Aõ," he reiterated again, making a kicking motion in her direction.

The girl called Aõ smiled at his attempt at humour and he laughed loudly at his own joke as he headed to his post.

She would have to wait until the guards changed over before she could make her escape.

Aõ bunkered down in the pretence of sleep. At the thought of her journey in the morning, the feeling of excitement began building like a kaleidoscope of butterflies flitting around deep in her stomach, keeping her from settling, her mind racing. She thought over each step of her first solo hunting expedition, a forbidden excursion not only for youngsters but, particularly, for women. She rehearsed her travel plans again and again just in case she missed some vital aspect. She worked out every possible ending and strategized every possible outcome. She was confident she covered all her bases.

Aõ blinked the sleep from her eyes as the feel of the light of the new day hit her through the small cracks in the wall. Stretching her arms and legs, she could feel her nervousness growing. Her hands had developed a slight tremor in the last couple of days as her adrenaline began to course through her body as her plans became a reality. The old ladies in charge of the girls missed nothing. If they saw a change in her manner, a change in her posture or behaviour, they would spot it and grow suspicious.

She was mindful that a daytime disappearance could be ignored but missing at night and for the evening meal would not.

The old ladies would put her truancy missing presence during the day to childish games being played with friends to whittle away the hours.

At fifteen seasons almost ready to enter womanhood, she really was considered too mature to engage in day time child games, when her time and energy should have been put to contributing to the needs of the tribe gathering food, meal preparation, cleaning, repairing damaged paneling to the huts, or mending clothing.

Therefore, she would be chastised—be put to work at some menial task that would take all day. There would also be a search party before evening fell if she did not hurry.

Despite these thoughts, this wasn't the primary cause of Aõ's anxiety; what distressed her most would be the missed opportunity to prove her worth—that she was capable of more than the menial woman's work—that she was something special, just as the stories foretold. The girl slipped out silently into the early morning.

#

It was midmorning when Aõ found her prey.

The mud squeezed cold and sticky between her toes as Aõ quietly eased her weight slowly forward, from the heel of her foot to the ball of her foot in anticipation of the next move she had to make. The muscles in her legs began a dull ache from being held in the same position for so long but Aõ ignored it, peering between the leaves and branches eyeing off the prey that Aõ knew would be hers alone in the taking. Breathing deep through her nostrils—even breaths so as not to disturb the air around her, she flexed her arm, her green eyes tracking the body movements of her target. With a quick jerk, the stone flew from the sling sharp and direct towards the small fat feathered body of the black pigeon. The bird's head flicked up in fright, wings outstretched ready for flight. As it launched from the branch it had been feeding on, the sharp stone found its mark beneath the deep plumage, fracturing the delicate keel in the bird's chest, driving sharp splinters of bone into the small quivering heart. The fat bird fell from the branch to lie still on the floor of the forest.

Aõ leapt up in joy; she had done it, her first kill with her new tool. She had done it by herself. Made the tool, planned the kill, tracked her prey, and waited with patience. All the weeks of planning had led her to this point. All by herself. Aõ felt herself stand straighter as her heart filled with joy and laughter bubbled up. With a guttural cry, she leaped up, arm held high with her hunting tool, celebrating her kill under the thick forest canopy of branches—Aõ was a hunter and just as good as the others, she could prove it now.

Aõ collected her pigeon, stroking the glossy soft feathers back and forth, running them through her fingers in admiration, the grin never leaving her face. How her heart swelled with pride as she imagined presenting to the weavers the glossy feathers to add to their creative work.

Aõ dug her fingers into the body to assess the meat content.

It pleased her immensely thinking how delighted her foster mother, Warea, would be, to have this added to the evening meal. The bird's flesh, especially the section over the breast, would yield a tasty, sweet meat. It might even make it on the chief's platter, she thought excitedly.

Aõ leant down closely to examine the condition of the bird's beak, turning the bird's head from side to side. These birds had long, black hooked beaks designed to dip deep into the yellow flowers to extract the nectar droplets that gather deep in the heart of the flowers. A shiny, hard beak, one that spoke of health and vitality, therefore, a young bird, she surmised. If there was one, then there would be more young birds, too. More for her to practice her tool on. Aõ grinned to herself in happiness at these thoughts and then moved to examine the bird further.

Her fingers stroked the hard claws flicking the talon with her fingernails. The claws and beak would be used by Ahan, the medicine man, for his concoctions and tonics to cure ailments.

They will celebrate her kill and see that she is not a burden but an asset to their tribe. Maybe then they would reconsider the recent suggestion of offering her up into slavery with the Grey Stone Tribe. The girl stopped grinning at this thought and the deep knot of anxiety began a vortex of swirling acid in her stomach. She would not dwell on this thought now, she decided. She would not let it intrude and ruin her day—a day that had taken much stealth, time, and preparation.

#

This morning's journey brought her much farther into the forest than necessary to make her first kill. It had taken all of the sun's movement, until it was high in the sky to get to the forest range where the yellow berry tree grew that was favoured by the black wood pigeons and giant avians that patrolled the forests.

Aõ was careful to tread lightly to not attract the attention of the giant birds she could see through the trees grazing on the sweet grass of the lower grasslands. She was not fearful of them, but certainly wary that her presence might disturb their feeding.

Aõ saw the giant birds in vast flocks and, many times, she hid under wet leaf litter to disguise her scent, lying beneath logs to watch fascinated at their mannerisms and study their behaviours intently.

They were exactly as described by the hunters—huge, black-feathered birds. Around their avian face, glossy blue iridescent skin that changed colour in the sun as they flicked their heads from side to side in response to any small cracking of branches, the calling of other birds and animals and, in particular, the melodic sounds of human voices.

Twelve feet tall when it stretched its neck, with long black-grey feathers and limbs ending with dagger-like talons on both feet.

No longer able to fly due to their huge size, these birds relied on speed, claws, and a pack-like mentality to survive.

It was known amongst all the tribes that these birds would eat predominantly shrubs, grasses, and tree matter, but they would also consume meat, including man flesh. The birds were called "Moa" by the hunters and they were a prized source of food and resources. One felled bird could feed and supply a tribe with resources of meat, feathers, and sinew for clothing and fat for cooking for many months.

Aõ heard of the tales of how the bird strategically hunted in flocks, deliberately separating the hunters to isolate them. They were huge, strong, and incredibly intelligent.

The girl also saw the deceased bodies of the unlucky hunters who had not been eaten by the birds being carried back into camp, sometimes in pieces, by the survivors of a failed hunt.

Disembowelled and shredded beyond recognition, the bodies would be laid out for burial, covered from top to bottom in woven flax, hidden from sight under the mats to hide the terrible shredding the corpse had sustained from the loved ones who came to mourn them.

An unsuccessful hunt was scrutinised by the hunters, elders, ladies, and warriors from all angles. The hunters would act out the chase, gesturing, pointing, and demonstrating the hunt for all to see. How they had herded and separated the flock, thrusting javelins and long pointed shafts in a mock display.

The loss of a hunter, especially a skilled hunter, was a terrible loss for the tribe. There would now be a family without a man to provide for them, now having to rely on the generosity of the tribe. The elder council and hunters would debate the setting of the trap and argue for days over the strategies used, mapping out the terrain, and working out what changed. Was it the hunting ground they chose? Maybe the hunt strategies? Was it the correct trap? Was it strong enough? Were the straps still strong? Were their javelins pointed enough?

The hunters themselves—their strengths and weaknesses, their placement in the hunt and their roles within the team.

Even the bird behaviour's and body language were discussed to work out what went wrong. Nothing was left to chance and it was very rare that a hunt failed a second time in the same way.

#

Now it was closer to dark at the end of the day, the sun was past its zenith and making its journey down the other side of its arc, and she needed to hurry—she backed away from where Aõ watched the giant birds and picked up the pace of her trot, weaving around the trees, ducking under low lying branches.

Aõ recognised the shapes appearing through the thinning trees as she neared the outer edge of the forest. The jut of the hill that marked the first sentry's post came into view. She stopped suddenly and ducked low in case she was seen.

Aõ could run like the wind when she felt like it. But today, it was the tightly wound ball of anxiety churning like a maelstrom of vomit in the pit of her stomach that drove her to run. Sure-footed with a sound judgement and decisive of where to place her feet. Which log to stand on, which one to leap over.

Aõ was fearful of her future. Desperate to get home now to quell the voices that supported the decision to remove her from the tribe. The faster she could get back, the faster she could show her worth.

#

The suggestion of her removal, in exchange for a newly confirmed master stone carver, was aired some weeks previously.

He was looking to set up his own stone carving trade in another tribe and, at this moment, the Emerald Water Tribe only had one stone master carver.

Aõ felt the suggestion growing with strength every day. She had never given it a thought until her name and status began to be discussed amongst the women and the suggestion of tribal transfer was pitched to the council.

Aõ had always believed that her standing and familial status in the tribe would protect her from such movements. It was an immensely distressing situation to find herself in.

She found herself breathing harder, her throat turned immediately dry and unable to swallow, as if a ball of pain had lodged itself in her throat, tears easing into her eyes.

Aõ could not believe that her life was considered so worthless to her foster mother, Warea, and her father figure, Ahan—those who had nurtured her to this point—that they would transfer her out to another tribe. It was a painful awakening into adulthood.

Whenever this thought slipped to the surface of her mind, she clutched nervously at the edge of her skirt like a child, palms sweaty when the chief's guards walked by, convinced that it was the day they were coming to inform her that the details of the transfer were completed, to pack up her belongings and get ready to leave the only home she had known.

#

Aõ had seen many tribal exchanges with varying degrees of happiness as the tribe strengthened areas of skills through the adoption of new members and the release of other members. They came with gifts of wooden carvings, local foods from their regions, woven blankets, necklaces of shells, and, most importantly, animals for food and breeding.

Aõ never gave much thought about the people and who the exchange was happening to. How the new members felt leaving behind their loved ones to start afresh in a place with strange people with different practices.

It was this anxiety-provoking proposition in mind that spurred her decision to build the tool she contemplated to help project her aim and strengthen her throw so she could hit a target at force.

She carefully began her planning a few weeks earlier, taking titbits of food to the wood carvers and water to ease their thirst as she made her way quietly around, scraping up the shavings and tidying their work area unobtrusively.

Aõ cautiously eyed the off cuts that fell to the floor from the carvers' work benches or were tossed haphazardly aside due to a minute defect spotted by the master carvers.

These she took for herself, secreted away in her garb to be worked on in her own time.

It had taken some time and bartering of food and labouring to get enough materials that were light to handle and enhance her throwing capacity.

In the pretence of gathering herbs or berries for the evening meal, Aõ would leave the compound every day to journey to the lower fields, away from prying, disapproving eyes, to practice her throws, build up the accuracy of the shot, and strengthen the power of her shots. This was just the start of her plans if this tool worked, she decided. Next, she would need to build a javelin to fit her size. Placid pigeons were one thing. Giant birds and crazed miniature boars were another.

#

Aõ kept running, dodging low to miss the branches, stepping high to jump the fallen logs. This she could do forever. She could see everything; she knew where to put her feet.

No one and nothing could catch her in full flight.

Now it was the final stretch of her excursion to get home. The sentries would not hesitate to give her a good cuffing around the ears regardless of whose lineage she stemmed from. They would blame the reddening of her face on a lie of her falling or something similar.

If Fat Knuckles were on duty, she could expect more than a headcuff.

Fat Knuckles would knock the wind from her and leave as many bruises as he could that would not be seen beneath her clothes. He did that enough times already.

Despite his size and age, he liked hurting her. Aõ could see it in his eyes, the widening of his pupils and the smirk on his mouth when an opportunity to trip, punch, or stab her became available. Sneaking out and going missing for an entire day was forbidden for any female; especially one that had not yet turned. Especially one that looked as unusual as her with her green eyes.

#

Making herself as small as possible, she began to climb the wall heading for the small breach in the cliff face one hundred meters above her, where the fence and the stone face started.

Unable to anchor the fence pallets securely to the stone wall and relying on its difficult ingress at ground level, the tribe sentries had all but forgotten to patrol this side of the fortifications. For an agile, small, single climber, it was a long, tiring climb but an easy one.

A weak point in their tribe's safety, the girl noted.

If she were chief, she would be doubling the guard at this point and teaching the warriors how to climb, grapple, throw and thrust javelin. She would find a way to reinforce the security on this side. As far as Aõ was concerned, it was pointless to concentrate all their strength on the front of the fortress. If there was a raid, the raiders would not be announcing themselves by coming down a well-known path. They would find a weakness, just as she had.

It was a different story, however, on the inside.

Aõ would have to dodge half a dozen guards to get safely into the kitchen, where she could lose herself amongst the hustle and bustle of meal preparations.

She could find Warea and show her the wood pigeon. From this point, it would all be perfect.

Aõ would not need to say any more or do anything else, as the girl knew Warea would loudly congratulate her and make sure everyone admired her kill.

Warea would speculate on who would benefit from the gift of pigeon.

Aõ also knew Warea would conveniently ignore how she obtained the pigeon and would refrain from mentioning time gone, how she killed it, and what she used.

This would be for the hunters to discuss with the girl later.

#

The girl caught her breath as she reached the top of the cliff, hauling herself up the last crag. Aõ lay still for a few minutes to regain her composure and give the colour to her face a chance to regain normalcy before she moved off.

Hunched over, hiding her face, she made it past the first two guards before a loud voice rang out across the field, stopping her in her tracks.

"Aõ." The girl stopped, hesitated, and glanced furtively up before shuffling forward again.

"Oh no," she whispered under her breath, "It's Little Big Boy." She clenched her eyes together in frustration.

Of all the people to see her at this time, it would have to be Little Big Boy.

"Aõ," he called again as he ran breathlessly up to her in his funny little skip run and continued to skip run as he tried to keep up with her.

"Be quiet, you noisy pig face," Aõ hissed back at him as she picked up her walking pace. Now afraid he would bring unwanted attention in her direction.

"Go away," Aõ interjected towards him.

"What's wrong, Aõ? Where have you been? Warea's been looking for you all day. I haven't seen you all day either, where were you?" Little Big Boy fired off his questions in rapid succession without a stop for breath.

Aõ peered down at him and her annoyance turned to humour. It was very rare that he couldn't put a smile on her face. Just being around him was like standing in a warm shaft of sunlight and the freshest air that made you smile for the joy of being alive.

Little Big Boy was tiny and rounded like pebbles stacked upon each other.

His little tummy rolls bounced up and down under the decorative jewellery around his neck, as he jiggled alongside her, attempting to keep up.

Rivets of sweat left run lines through the thin layer of dirt that encrusted his beaming face and down across his jiggling belly rolls. His hair was a mess, though she could see some attempt had been made to tie it back and random haphazard plaits of varying sizes were scattered throughout his hair.

His special stones and carved wooden trinkets swung from side to side, tied with a fine flax cord around his neck.

His furry rabbit loin cloth peeked in and out from under his belly as he walked-skipped next to her. "So where were you?" he asked again.

"Just around the place," she replied, "Getting something nice for the old lady and supplies for the weavers."

"Oohhhh, did you get one?" he asked, his eyes growing large as he reached out to pluck at her cloak.

Aõ smiled in response and ceased walking. "Look," she bent her head down and opened her satchel slightly to show Little Big Boy the beautiful plume of the feathers and the lifeless fat body of the wood pigeon.

"I got it on my first throw; the throwing tool works, Little Big Boy, and I knew it would." Aõ looked at him intensely and he stared back at her just as hard.

"I knew you could do it, Aõ. I knew you were magical."

Immediately, Aõ snatched the satchel closed and glared at him, "It wasn't magic, you stupid pig face, it was just me and my hard work." Aõ stomped off around the corner, glaring back at Little Big Boy and walked directly into the path of the young man she called Fat Knuckles.

"What are you doing?" Fat Knuckles demanded, placing one hand on her chest, grasping the shirt underneath, and twisting it into a lock hold. "What are you up to, scab?" he said as he pulled her in close to his face.

His two men at arms stood menacingly on either side of him, staring down at her, crossing their arms over their chest, and puffing themselves up to look bigger. They furtively began looking around to make sure no one could see them picking on a smaller, defenceless person as they moved into position to block the view of the standoff.

Little Big Boy's eyes grew wide, and he turned and ran.

#

Of all the annoying people around, Fat Knuckles hated this girl the most. Even when they were small children, he could not tolerate her. Aõ looked wrong. Her hair was the wrong colour—too similar to the light brown dirt that the pigs turned over when grubbing about for the soft, tender roots that grew close to the surface. Her hair should be glossy black like the other women's, reflective of the rich soils found in the forest that much of their staple food source came from.

Aõ smelt wrong to him, too sweet, like decomposing meat; she should smell earthy like the other women, he surmised, and her eyes, no one in this tribe or any other from neighbouring tribes had eyes that colour except Ahan, the medicine man. Divine birth orchestrated by Ahan in the barren second wife of the new chief, Amaro, was the story that surrounded her.

In the essence of his bones, he could feel that Aõ was different, and being different in Fat Knuckle's mind was the same as evil.

He took every opportunity to belittle her, undermine her integrity, and cast doubt on her character. If she walked past him on a task for the ladies, he would make disparaging comments about her to the other men, always linking it to her strange looks and supposed evil nature.

If a hunt went wrong, it was because Aõ had been too close to the hunting weapons during the preparation stage. If a food item spoilt, it was because Aõ must have touched it prior to cooking.

Fat Knuckle's aim was to hurt her, to make her hate it here, to drive her out and then he could protect his people from her.

The time would come very soon that he would not be able to physically hurt her anymore, which would have to cease once she became a woman, but he would find another way to get rid of her.

When he was chief, he would make sure Aõ was sold as a barren slave.

When he was chief, he could have her murdered for any indiscretion he could come up with.

#

He twisted his grip on her shirt tighter. "Answer me, you useless pig, what are you doing here in this place at this time, when you should be at food preparation?"

He spat the words out through clenched teeth.

He wished he could sink them into her cheek.

The girl looked calmly up at him and spat directly in his face. His eyes widened in disbelief, spit spraying from between his clenched teeth, infuriated at her insubordinate response.

He slammed his rock-hard fist into her face, splitting her cheek open. Still holding her in his tightly wound grip, he pulled his fist back again and punched Aõ hard in the stomach, causing her to exhale explosively as the air left her lungs.

Aõ's legs collapsed beneath her but, still, Fat Knuckles did not release his grip.

He smiled at his men enjoying the power he had over her now limp body, switching hands to now grip Aõ by the neck, pulling her up into a standing position, shaking her like a marionette doll.

"Who do you think you are? You are less than the shit that falls from the animal's arse. I will squash you into the ground at every opportunity; you are no match for me, and I will unmake you," he hissed in her face.

He glanced down at his free arm, admiring how his muscles in his arms flexed and bulged as he pulled his arm back in readiness.

His groin pulled and tightened, an outward projection of the excitement he was having at Aõ's expense. He marvelled at his strength, the beauty in himself, sending a thoughtful thank you to the ancient ones for giving him his perfectness.

Fat Knuckles glanced over to his comrades standing nervously off to one side, watching him and looking out across the compound in case they got caught.

Fat Knuckles was selective in his friendship group, selecting those young men he knew would follow his lead without question, choosing the young men that he could groom.

He eyeballed them one by one, waiting for them to acknowledge with a slight nod of their head or the glint of admiration in their eyes at his power, his strength, and his physique.

He stretched his fingers wide, closing them slowly in an exaggerated display of his intentions.

His fist smashed into Aõ's cheek causing the skin to split along the eye socket.

Fat Knuckles laughed in utter enjoyment of his power, feeling the grip of the loin cloth as it slid over and diagonally across his manhood, the hard fibres of the flax sliding on the perspiration that now dripped over his loins running down between his legs in the exertion of his punches.

As he hit Aõ in her stomach again and again, feeling the rising of excitement pulling in his crotch, his breath quickened as the rhythmic punching movements caused the rubbing of the loin cloth on his now stiffened cock as that became his focus as he edged towards release.

For Aõ, now semi-unconscious, the pain became a dull thud until, gratefully, sinking deep within herself, she could not feel or hear anything anymore.

# Chapter 2

# Lies Will Kill You

When she woke, Aõ could feel herself on a soft bed of fresh brambles covered by a blanket made of coarse black boar hair and countered with the soft under-down feathers of pigeons cleverly woven and linked together on the underside. Small glimpses of light fell on her face and through the slats of tree fern poles cleverly linked together to block out the cold but allow healing light to filter through. Aõ knew where she was, she had been here enough times already in her short fifteen years of life. She was amazed she still lived. She wondered how bad she was this time. If Fat Knuckles was finally able to break some bones, make her unsatisfactory as a wife or slave. Damage her woman's parts so she would be unable to breed and be, therefore, unappealing except as a slave.

She became aware of something pressing uncomfortably into the back of her skull keeping her head and shoulders rigid.

Aõ attempted to tentatively move. Immense pain shot through her neck, radiating in hot bursts down her arms and into the small of her back. Aõ cried out in pain; tears began rolling down her face, as she whimpered herself back into stillness.

"It hurts!" she called out.

"Ahan, she's awake," a young woman's anxious voice called out.

"My name is Mara; do you remember me?" she asked as she patted Aõ in sympathy. "Ahan said not to move or breathe deeply either. The bones on the inside of you are very broken and pointy and may poke a hole in you elsewhere," Mara's flute-like voice was confident in the instructions she gave.

"You must drink this, try and urinate, you did yesterday when you were asleep, and it came out red. Ahan is worried about you. He doesn't say, but I can tell, in his face and movements, he thinks you may die and go to the ancient ones," Mara stated in a matter-of-fact manner, her expression was one of indifference towards whether Aõ lived or died.

"He says you had a really bad fall and that you are lucky you didn't die." Mara's little pixie face nodded up and down as she looked at Aõ in doubt as she spoke.

#

Mara's hair was plaited in multiple even braids and woven into a formal bun at the back of her head, indicative of the role and responsibilities of an acolyte—a trainee in medicine.

At the young age of sixteen years, Mara's arms and chin had already been tattooed to display her learning.

As expected, Mara had very few body adornments, unlike many of the women in the tribe; another indicator of not needing material possessions to advertise her value, rather, Mara's markings gave an esoteric display of her worth and how much she had progressed in the arcane world of medicine and magic.

Mara held up a small, beautifully carved cup to Aõ's lips, encouraging her to take a sip. Aõ sipped at the medicine, barely able to raise her head to get the fluid in.

Aõ swallowed with difficulty, the painful ache of her crushed throat causing her to grimace. The cuts stung as the bitter concoction ran over her lips.

"You look so funny," the young girl observed. "Papa had to reset your nose and paste your face back together, too. You are red and white coloured like a strange beast,"

"You really are very lucky that you survived the fall," the girl prattled on as she fussed around straightening the pillow and blanket. "Not many people could survive a tumble that far."

So, Fat Knuckles had thrown me back down the cliff, thought Aõ. This would have covered the damage that he inflicted on her.

This time he made a serious attempt to kill her. It would not be easy to assign blame to Fat Knuckles for her injuries.

He was getting clever in disguising his assaults.

Aõ ran her tongue around the inside of her mouth. All her teeth appeared intact, though some felt painfully loose as she probed. The skin inside her mouth was torn from where Fat Knuckles slammed her face—her tongue felt ragged and ached on the sides from the splits that had opened under the brutal pounding she received.

"Yes, I am lucky," Aõ croaked back in response.

The acolyte looked up with an incredulous expression on her face.

"We know that you did not get your injuries from a fall but were given to you by someone's fists. Why do you hide behind a lie?" Mara enquired, disbelieving that someone would not admit the reasons for the damage done to their body.

Tears eased out from Aõ's eyes and a painful lump grew in the back of her throat. How could she explain to Mara the inherent hatred that Fat Knuckles had for her, for things that looked different in his eyes—like her—meant danger to him?

For behaviours that did not fit with his version of the women's role were anticipated as a threat.

#

Aõ could not see the sense of why the boundaries of female and male roles existed. It was something she struggled with all her short life, exacerbated by her early introduction into the men's learning as well as that of the women's.

If boys could be taught to fight at an early age, why not the girls and double the number of warriors and hunters?

Why not teach the men to forage and grow foods? This, in Aõ's mind, meant twice as many gatherers for the seasonal harvests.

These were the thoughts and ideas she voiced at a council meeting one evening a few years earlier, ideas that were laughed at by many in the room and treated with gentle condescension by the elders.

Fat Knuckles, however, sitting amongst his group of male cronies, leaned forward, glaring at her. "She should not be allowed to speak, she should not even be in here!" he yelled aggressively at the elders, pointing directly at her. Aõ shrunk back in fear after her outburst to hide behind Warea, mindful that she had just given Fat Knuckles another reason for a beating.

The elders focused on his distress, had calmed Fat Knuckle's outburst with soothing words, reminding him that anyone could speak to improve the functioning of the tribe but not at the expense of traditions; traditions from the old world and now, the new world were not up for debate, it was definitive that they were not subject to change.

Despite this, Fat Knuckles continued to glare his hatred across at Aõ for the remainder of the evening, spitting in distaste in her direction whenever the conversation drifted to speakers who sat nearby.

Aõ, however, sat, head down, face flamed with the heat of embarrassment at her boldness to speak out and did not speak further.

Aõ knew Fat Knuckles interpreted her as a stain, from the awakening of her awareness as a baby, she knew he hated her. She had spent her entire childhood evading his attention.

Her comments regarding a break in the way of traditions, would be considered by Fat Knuckles as imminent death for the tribe. For what Fat Knuckles saw in Aõ's concept of inclusive life, was the death of their culture that extended before their life and beyond their time.

#

The small medicine girl waited and, seeing that no answer was forthcoming, wiped the tears from Aõ's eyes and got to her feet.

"Your lie will kill you next time. You had better learn to come up with some truths if you want to live."

Mara turned, eyeballing Aõ as she walked from the room, disappearing from Aõ's immediate sight.

#

# Chapter 3

# Ahan - His Story

The divider was held respectfully open by Mara to allow her master, Ahan, to step into the small bedroom space. The man that entered was impressive and very obviously not native to this tribe.

In contrast to the Emerald people's looks, Ahan's nose was straight and austere.

Ahan's skin was a lightly coloured brown. His face was broad, yet it sported finely chiselled cheekbones and jawline. His face looked fierce beneath the intricate layers of mystical symbols tattooed on his face and body.

Tattoo designs chosen with care to showcase his magical prowess of the physical and spiritual worlds that he, Ahan, the medicine man, was in sync with.

He looked nothing like the men of this tribe, even though his tattoos declared him to be. Dark brown skin, jet black glossy hair, broad-faced with flatter noses, thick lips, and bulky muscular torsos with an average size of six foot seven inches, was the common look of the Green Emerald Water Tribe.

The Medicine Man's build at six foot two was smaller than the men of the tribe, but his firm, tight-muscled chest, arms, and thighs rippled and radiated physical and inner strength more than any member..

His body tattoos appeared to move along his limbs at will, snaking up and down, dependant on how he chose to display them, coiling in his biceps in readiness for potential exertion, curling and concentrated in astral power in his thighs in anticipation of release.

Each tattoo was designed to enhance the power that resided in that area of his body.

He allowed his hair to grow long over the winter, caramel brown with sun-bleached streaks; there was no disguising he was not native to the tribe.

Unashamed of its colour or guise, he wore it shaved on both sides so that it could be woven in a single plait through the centre of his head or have it hang loose, falling on either side of his head, as he had it now. A casual display rather than a ceremonial style.

Ahan stepped forward, looking down to appraise Aõ's condition. His much thinner lips were now pursed in introspect.

Like Aõ, Ahan had the same green eyes. But, unlike Aõ, he was revered throughout all the tribes as the most powerful medicine man.

Ahan was renowned for his many skills, one, in particular, was enticing the gods to bring forth whatever the Emerald Water Tribe needed at that time.

#

"Hello, Aõ. I am pleased to see you are awake," said Ahan as he came into the room to stand at the side of her bed. Aõ peered up at him through swollen eyes.

Ahan knelt by the bed, lifting Aõ's head gently. "You must drink more of this; it will help with the pain."

With difficulty, Aõ swallowed the concoction Ahan offered.

"Ahan, my satchel, did anyone find my satchel?" she whispered.

Ahan nodded definitively once, "That is another matter that will need to be discussed at another more appropriate time."

Aõ, confused at his response, reached out painfully and gently grasped his arm.

"What is wrong Ahan?" she rasped.

Ahan took a deep breath blowing gently out his nostrils wondering how much he should tell her.

"We found you a short way down the cliff. The guards that accompanied us found the sacred green stone in your satchel. They are saying that you stole the green stone back and tried to leave by scaling down the cliff face. They claim you must have lost your footing and fell when you were trying to escape."

Ahan gently placed his hand on hers and shook his head.

"Do not worry about this, Aõ. When you are well enough, you will have the opportunity to tell your side of the story."

"Guards are known for the strength of arm, not their strength of mind."

Ahan gently patted her hand and laid it back on the bed.

"You must rest now."

Aõ swallowed and minutely nodded her head in acknowledgement.

Fat knuckles' web of lies and assaults were tightening around her. She could almost feel it.

He or his cronies stole the sacred green stone and planted it on her. Switching it for her wood pigeon—her first kill—and more than likely claimed it was a kill they made.

With her being incapacitated, Fat Knuckles had the time and enough listening ears to spread his angst against her.

Desperate to not be alone with her bitter ruminations, Aõ called out in anguish.

"Please do not leave me just yet, Ahan. Tell me again how you came to be here. Tell me about the wayfarers' journey. Tell me why you had to leave the first home."

Ahan smiled at her, knowing it was a decoy distraction but happy to recount this for her—his first born.

As he examined Aõ, he could see the indentations of where fists had hit her and bruising that matched the shape of fingers around her neck. He struggled to contain his rage at the desecration of Aõ's body by Rimachi, known by Aõ as Fat Knuckles, the son of the current chief, Amaro, and Ahan's bosom brother.

#

If it had not been for Little Big Boy alerting him to the assault, she would have died before she was found.

Little Big Boy burst into the healing hut, waving his hands around and yelling hysterically about Fat Knuckles hitting Aõ behind the outer houses. Ahan and his acolytes dropped what they were doing and immediately followed Little Big Boy in haste to where he had left Aõ in the grips of Fat Knuckles.

By the time they got to her, Fat Knuckles and his men had already tossed her casually over the cliff and were walking away as if nothing happened.

Little Big Boy, having seen the direction they were walking from, ran immediately over to the fence, climbing through the rails to peer anxiously through the darkness over the side.

Ahan strode with determined steps toward the last place Little Big Boy had seen Aõ. He spotted the three men sauntering away casually. "Rimachi," called out Ahan.

The young man called Fat Knuckles by Aõ stopped and sneered at Ahan with barely concealed hostility before bowing his head in sarcastic respect.

"Yes, Honoured One? Is there something I can help you with?'

Ahan acknowledged Rimachi in return with a similar head bow.

"Yes, Rimachi, there is," replied Ahan, "I am looking for Aδ. Little Big Boy tells me she was with you a few moments ago," asked Ahan, seeing Rimachi swallow in a brief moment of doubt.

Rimachi, with his elegantly shaved head and face sculptured in the style of geometric shapes designed to enhance his jaw in sharp angles, opened his eyes wide in mock surprise and shook his head from side to side in denial.

"She walked past us, Honoured One, I did not see which direction she left in. I did not see where she went," he replied, shrugging his shoulders nonchalantly in an attempt at ignorance.

At that moment, Little Big Boy, who had made his way tentatively down the precarious path, let out a screech, "I see something down here, come quickly,"

Rimachi placed his hand on his chest in a sign of submission. "Allow myself and my men to help, Honoured one, we will climb down to see what he has found,"

Rimachi pivoted quickly on his heel, signalling with a quick jerk of his fingers to his men to accompany him back to the fence.

It was here, under the close scrutiny of Ahan, his caregivers, and Little Big Boy, that Aδ's damaged, almost lifeless body was hauled back up the cliff.

The fat pigeon in Að's satchel was gone and, in its place, the sacred green stone, the most treasured heart stone of the Emerald Water Tribe was discovered.

#

# Chapter 4

# An Unnatural Aversion

Ahan could see she needed to have her mind turned to something other than her current worries.

To let Aõ stress at this time of healing would do more damage to her spirit, maybe even to the point where she would not want to recover.

Ahan felt deep regret for Aõ and, again, wondered how his miracle baby could turn out to be so wonderful and yet be treated with such mistrust by her own tribe. It was not her fault. This he knew.

He watched her from a distance every day, observing all her moves from a small babe to a young girl. She had done nothing to warrant such suspicion and had always demonstrated excellent behaviour.

Aõ was quick to learn. Athletic, fair in her play, never shucked her duties. Aõ was polite and respectful to the elders, ladies, and visitors.

Ahan knew there were whispers of her spirit being not right but Ahan had not been able to pinpoint when it had started and from whom these rumours were perpetuating.

Ahan himself could not see or tap into what was wrong with her inner spirit. It did not feel wrong to him. To Ahan, Aõ was important in the survival of the tribe. She was a gift from the gods, not a curse.

Ahan did recognise, however, Rimachi's aversion to Aõ.

Ahan had seen, even as small children, Rimachi deliver spiteful punches—when he thought no one was watching—hair pulls and upsetting of Aõ's games that many adults just put down to childish pranks, and Ahan thought the same for many years.

But, as the years went past and the other boys grew out of their perpetual torment of the girls into a fascination with them, Rimachi, however, did not show this inclination towards Aõ or any other female.

Ahan watched on and, as Rimachi grew bigger, Ahan's quiet observations turned to horror as Rimachi's assaults became fiercer.

But there was little Ahan could do for the girl, given the tribal position of Rimachi and who his father was.

When Aõ reached the age of womanhood, Ahan approached Warea, Aõ's carer, with the blunt opening of, "We must talk about Aõ and her position." He stared off into the distance, strangely uncomfortable with interfering with the woman's business and how this exchange should take place.

"Yes, Honoured One?" replied Warea.

That evening, after the women and children had cleared the shared evening meals, in a quiet corner of the big house, Warea placed cushions of softened woven flax stuffed with pigeon feathers down on the mat for her and Ahan to sit on.

The remaining people in the house courteously avoided the two as they deciphered that a private conversation was about to be undertaken between Ahan and Warea.

Warea poured two cups of warm peppermint tea for them both, the aroma of the tea settling their nerves as they both looked for ways to speak about Aõ and the problems she was encountering.

"I know what it is that you wish to speak to me about," nodded Warea, eventually pulling her cloak closer around her shoulders.

"I too have seen the assaults Rimachi is inflicting on our Aõ; because of his status, it has been hard for me not to strike the boy in anger," she admitted with eyes downcast.

Ahan nodded at her in acknowledgement and continued to sip thoughtfully on his tea as she spoke.

"Ahan, I am worried for her safety and, if we do not intervene, Rimachi will damage her enough that she will have no worth, miracle baby or not," she stated in earnest.

Ahan nodded once in acknowledgement of the truth of her statements.

Ahh, he thought, Warea has seen and has the same concerns as me. Sitting in silence, allowing Warea's statements to gain strength, now spoken aloud in the night and now under their consideration.

Ahan sipped his tea slowly, enjoying the flavours running across his tongue as he finished the last dregs.

Warea sat respectfully, waiting for Ahan's response. Her increased breathing was the only outward sign of her anxiousness regarding the outcome of the medicine man's deliberations.

Ahan looked thoughtfully at Warea. "My thoughts are to remove her from the children's groups and place her into the adult groups. That way, Rimachi is unable to gain access to her without an adult being around," responded Ahan.

Warea smiled, nodding her head in gratitude at the wisdom of Ahan's decision.

She knew he had given Aõ the best chances of surviving and adding value to her worth, regardless of whether she could breed or not.

A girl that could work the growing and harvest seasons, anticipate the movements and behaviours of small animals, set traps, and prepare meals would still be valued by any tribe. Aõ would not be without worth.

"Thank you, Honoured One, as always, you know what is needed to ensure the safety of the tribe," responded Warea.

Warea, tempted to push Ahan's good will, contemplated asking Ahan about reprimanding Rimachi. As she sought the words, Ahan abruptly added to his one sentence.

"We cannot touch him; he is not ours to correct." With his head tilted introspectively to one side, Ahan added,

"Though the boy would benefit from a good whipping and thumping by someone bigger than him."

They both smiled at each other in camaraderie in this statement, wishing it could be so.

Ahan suddenly added, "You must prepare yourself in case this plan does not have the outcome we are wanting. It will only protect Aõ until she becomes a woman, Rimachi may have had his status elevated before then. If this is the case, then Aõ will again be at risk, a greater risk," reiterated Ahan, "And it will mean we will need to send Aõ out of the tribe and into another."

It was on the awakening of the next day that Warea and Ahan began the attempt to put distance between the two children.

Warea drew Aõ into the fold of the ladies, having her commence the tasks of homecare, medicine, weaving, and cooking at a much earlier age than most. The fact that Aõ was so young to be engaging in these higher-skilled activities was not lost on the elder ladies.

But, amongst the ladies at least, it was the belief that Aõ was a gift from the gods and that alone held the ladies tongues from speaking out against Aõ's inclusion.

It was a different story with the men and it was with greater scrutiny and open hostility by the men that Aõ was allowed to sit out of sight and unable to speak but begrudgingly included in the deliberations, debating and observations of the warriors, hunters, and the strategizing of foraging. It was purely that Aõ had been introduced as being under the protection of Ahan that stopped open rebellion from occurring.

Aõ was fascinated with the strategizing of the hunts and the delicate art of tribal negotiations for people, food, and equipment.

She would sit quietly absorbing all as the men discussed hunting strategies. Aõ began to see in her mind's eye the lay of the land, the terrain and waterways, animal trails, and their ways of hiding in the undergrowth.

Aõ paid particular attention to the discussions and debate around the internal functioning of holding an emerging culture together—built from the remnants of the old world—with that of a new world, with a multitude of people from various islands and cultures.

"If all the men could have her studious nature," thought Ahan, "Our tribe would be the strongest of all."

#

Ahan smiled, "Okay, Aõ, I will tell you some of our story," he replied. Ahan's eyes closed as he began his recount of the most influential and revered person of the Emerald Water Tribe.

# Chapter 5

# The Old Chief of the Old World

"The old chief was called Mateo," began Ahan.

"He had travelled enough throughout his years, visited many tribes as he was expected to during his reign to forge ongoing alliances.

"His peaceful delegations had roamed far and wide across the broad mountain ranges and down deep into the jungle forests. Meeting small villages, exchanging gifts and bartering foods, relearning the generation changes to hierarchy and re-establishing familial lineages. It was during the travels along the furthest coastal plains that Mateo had seen for himself the strange floating vessels on the water. Huge monstrosities in comparison to his tribe's small wave riders. Even from his position on the ridge in the bright sun, the vessels far out to sea were massive. The old chief could not believe what he was seeing. If a scout had tried to describe the size to him, he would not have believed it. Mateo would have sent the man away with a laugh.

"A careful, discreet man, his delegation refrained from investigating further. He had fathomed for himself that a vessel of that size would have many men to manage it and, therefore, considered that it was here to bring much or here to take much. It was something he had to watch from afar."

Að nodded her head in acknowledgement. "Yes, it would have been unnerving to see crafts like that on the water," she commented, eyes wide in interest at Ahan's historical account.

Ahan adjusted his position slightly on the stool and continued his story.

"Over the years that came, Mateo sent scouts out to the East over the mountains and North up the coast with the objective to listen and watch, with an aim to gather information exclusively on the big vessels and on those that sailed them.

"On return, the scouts would report to Mateo.

"Mateo, sitting in a fur-lined chair, thoughtfully staring into the fire, watching the flames flick and burn the sturdy logs, he would begin his questioning.

"Tell me which route you took," Mateo would begin, looking to hear the scout describe the terrain, direction, and distance he travelled. Mateo, familiar with these journeys, nodded his head in recognition as the scout spoke of familiar landmarks that distinguished the border territories of the many tribes within the land.

"My chief," the scout would respond in respect, "I travelled for fifty days north over the dividing mountains and inland to the outer reaches of the thick jungles marked by the swollen tree of ages that hangs its fruit over the river."

"It was after five days of travel out to the coast, that I came across the village of the Redwood Tribe and signs that the ghosts had been amongst them," continued the scout.

"What signs make you believe the ghosts had been there?" retorted Mateo.

"The scout, familiar with this line of questioning, began preparing his statement of evidence.

"My chief, I disguised myself in clothing of the Redwood Tribe; I noticed that many of the campfires were dead, many people were missing. I spoke with an old man of the Redwood Tribe who described how the healthy women, older children, and men had been beaten, chained, and herded away. He did not know where they were being taken. Those people of the Redwood Tribe that resisted were murdered by the ghosts—where they stood was where they died. There were not enough healthy men left in the Redwood Tribe to bury the dead, my chief," recounted the scout, choking back his anguish at the brutal sights he had seen.

"The bodies of women, men and children were left to rot in the heat, in the open," continued the Scout.

"I stayed, my chief, to help those left with the burials—there were not enough people left, my chief, the Redwood Tribe will be no more," the scout whispered, staring at the ground blankly.

"You did the Redwood Tribe a great honour and I am proud of your graciousness to help. It was a task you did not have to do and yet you did. I am proud you are part of The Emerald Water Tribe," responded Mateo, aware of the distress the scout encountered.

"Go, now, see your family, eat, and recover, I will not need you for some time. When you are well and rested, you may come to me again for your next mission," replied Mateo, dismissing the scout with a clap on his shoulder and a wave for him to leave.

"The scout nodded his head, respectfully bowed, and backed away from the chief.

"Mateo returned to his ponderings. His hair, now salt and pepper coloured and shaved on one side, was left long. It was woven in numerous thick braids carefully sculpted around the tattoos on his scalp, giving depth and definition to the markings that advertised his status. Mateo's body was becoming soft with age and the lack of physical assertions of daily wrestling, hunting, and spear practice that he now left for the younger men to engage in.

"The accounts from the scouts returning to the safety and isolation of the Emerald Water Tribe territory were recounting the same stories he had heard filtering back to him from across the land. It was clear to the old chief that these ghosts and the vessels he had seen, were harbingers of doom.

"Many of the scouts did not come back and the few that did spoke of strange men-like creatures with white skin, strange clothing and languages. They took what they wanted, including women and children, killed who they wanted with no apparent value for life.

"Other scouts spoke of illnesses that wiped out entire villages, leaving few survivors and those surviving being left weak and sick, like poorly formed newborns and scarred beyond recognition.

"These things were recounted to Mateo by his scouts who were sworn to silence. Mateo did not want his precious tribe to hear of these things. It was inevitable that, soon, someone would hear a whisper through the trees, see these ghosts as they made their way closer.

"Until that time, Mateo had to have a script of words and a plan of action ready."

#

"The chief's plan was agonisingly loose and poorly formed at best; he knew this.

"Fight, do nothing, or run.

"The old chief heard and saw for himself what happened to tribes that tried the first two options. These options were death. Then that left to run. Where to? Where was safe? Where could they go that the ghosts could never find them? All the lands were divided carefully amongst the overlords for generations.

"The boundary markers of mountain ranges, flowing waterways, and deep ravines had kept tribes peaceful and prosperous. One did not simply walk into another's land

and set up house. It had rarely been done outside of tribal families—but it had been done, considered Mateo.

"He did not relish giving up his status and bountiful lands of waterways forests and mountains—these lands had been in this tribe's hands for generations.

"The revered stone carvings of the ancients, the footprints of giant beings melted in rocks, and the beautiful colour and rich food sources of their river's water—this is what gave the Emerald Water Tribe their name and their high status.

"The old chief agonised and delayed his decision.

"How could he take his tribe away? Leave so much behind?

"The more Mateo considered leaving, the more reasons he found to stay—an impossible decision to be made.

"That was until the arrival of Maarkus and his baby."

# Chapter 6

# A Ghost, A Goat, and A Child

Ahan stood, stretching his back, and made his way to the small table to pour himself a drink of cool water and take a small handful of berries to eat whilst he continued his story.

"Mateo's scouts spotted the small vessel one morning making its zigzag way up one of the waterways a few weeks earlier

"There is a man with a babe and a small goat in the vessel, my chief," reported the scout.

"There is no one else," finished the scout. They watched as instructed by Mateo not to engage and to stay out of sight whilst feeding information back to the old chief on the small vessel's movements and that of the person in it.

"The scout recounted what the singular man carried and how his handling of the small watercraft with the river currents assisted to hasten his way.

"What is this man's rush? thought the old chief and he sat stirring the embers of the fire with his stick. Has he stolen the child he carries? The old chief sat up suddenly, pausing the stick in the embers He did!, He has stolen the child and now he's running away, why else would a single man, and a ghost at that, leave his people?

"He cares for this child", the chief surmised by the scout's daily reports of the ghost milking the small goat to feed the baby and stopping often to find food for the goat. The goat was a problem, the scouts reported another day, they noted how anxious the ghost man acted when the goat bleated loudly. Yes, thought the old chief, he has run away and he doesn't want to be found.

"As the daily reports filtered in, Mateo continued to build a picture of the circumstances around this little watercraft and the strange inhabitants on board.

"Mateo began stirring the embers with his stick faster as his thoughts moved towards barter and negotiations. "This is a gift," he decided.

"He had a ghost in his lands seeking solace, no doubt. We could turn this to our advantage, the ghost knows the ways of the ghost people, knows how to traverse water over great distances, he could teach us new ways, we could learn the ghosts' weaknesses. A slow smile crept over his face as he stared intently into the fire. Yes, I could learn much from him and, if he doesn't fit in, we will kill him, the old chief nodded at his decision.

"Stop staring like that, husband! You look like a crazed spirit!" the raspy voice of an old lady from the other side of the fire cut through his inner ramblings, making Mateo jump with fright.

"Do not interrupt me when I am meditating, old woman," he replied tersely to his wife, Ara. Irritated at Ara's interruption, he began poking vigorously at the fire again, wanting the feeling of mental triumph back.

"He glanced over at her, seeing the smirk of enjoyment on her face at his expense.

"Just once, he thought, I would like to enjoy my hubris, is that so wrong? He looked up in anticipation of shooting his wife a hateful glare, only to sit back in fright again at his wife's intense stare.

"It's a good plan, husband, a very good plan, we will win either way with this decision," said Ara in response to his shocked look.

"The hairs on Mateo's arms stood up, it made him extremely uncomfortable when his wife made these predictions, but he admitted she was never wrong.

"Mateo nodded in acknowledgement of her statement and Ara respectfully returned the gesture, turning her attention back to her grandson, Amaro, sleeping peacefully in her lap.

"He looked toward the door, raising his chin slightly, and the guard stepped forward, head bowed in respect. "Yes, my chief?"

"There is a ghost, a goat, and a child travelling up the Emerald River, make sure they arrive here safely. I want them treated as though they are of our tribe and members of my family. Do you understand?"

"The guard nodded. "Yes, my chief, not a hair on the head of the ghost, the goat, or the child will be harmed," he responded.

"Do not interfere with him but make sure he is gently guided here to me; assist with feeding and watering him, too.

"Show him we mean no harm," The old chief added as an afterthought.

"Yes, my chief," responded the guard. "We will guide them to you."

#

# Chapter 7

# Maarkus and His Baby

No one really knew where Ahan and his father, Maarkus, came from, only that they were not from any of the lands that the Emerald Water Tribe knew of. They only understood that Maarkus, with a baby strapped on his back, and in the company of a small wiry goat, had travelled furthest on water and land than anyone they knew of. Maarkus and his baby wandered into their tribal lands and were welcomed into the Emerald Water Tribe with little ado.

After the second night of discussions between the elders and Maarkus, it was decided he was a valuable asset in both knowledge and his physical capabilities, and they would protect him and the babe from those that sought him harm. He had also brought with him implements and weapons made of materials that no one had ever seen before but were instantly recognised by the elders as weapons of great meaning and strength.

It would be his influence all those long years ago that brought them to this place of safety in the clouds.

#

Maarkus was a man of little colour to his skin and had what the Emerald Water Tribe women described as hair that had the sun in it. He also had the eyes of a blind man but could still see. Greyish blue in colour which reflected stones in many women's eyes. He was not considered unattractive but not attractive either. His physique was considered small and compact, standing at a height of five foot eight inches with little muscle development compared to the dark-skinned, muscular men of the Emerald Water Tribe. Many men and young males turned it into a jest as they stood listening and watching Maarkus, busy with his map-making, pointing out key land masses. The young men would flex their bicep muscles, bounce their chest muscles up and down at each other whilst Maarkus was blissfully unaware, continuing on his teachings of stars, water, and the patterns found in each.

#

Ahan shifted on his stool, continuing his recount for Aõ, who he could see was swept up in the imagery of his storytelling.

"My father was always aware of the great risk he brought upon the Emerald Water Tribe when he found them.

"They were the most western tribe with wayfarer capabilities, and my father knew that it was just a matter of time before the rest of his people caught up with him.

"My father was also aware of the great generosity acceptance solace, and safety the old chief gave him, and in exchange, my father gave all the knowledge and survival skills he had on wayfaring.

"He was indebted to the old chief, Mateo, who had demonstrated so much foresight.

"A firm friendship developed quickly between the two men as they both anticipated the imminent arrival of the ghosts."

#

"He made sure to pass on his knowledge of the toolmaking and weaponry he had managed to escape with. Every day, he could be found waiting at the large grass area ready to show whoever was interested how to use the sharp metal blade in a variety of ways to assist with carving new items and how it could be used for digging, stabbing, and cutting pelts.

"When enough people tried this tool and learnt to make their own from lesser materials, he would move on to drawing maps in the sand, showing the outline of land masses with pebbles for hills and mountains, blades of grass for forests and sticks to show the different tribal groups.

"Some knowledge, however, he held off from sharing with all who were interested; this knowledge he only shared with the elders and those known as the wave riders, for this was considered knowledge of the gods.

"Many of the tribe struggled with the basic information.

"Maarkus shared. He would draw the same symbol or a sequence of symbols in the dirt and describe a word or sentence that was its meaning. Many people thought it was unbelievable—how could that symbol mean a mountain? A mountain was a thing you climbed, with trees and large rocks, or a bird. A bird was a moving animal with feathers and beak. How could it be this thing drawn on the ground, in sand?

"It was too far-fetched for many people to understand. They would laugh and they thought Maarkus and his ghost ways were placed in the realms of fantasy—childhood stories for telling on long nights to keep people amused.

"Others found his stories—the arrival of ghosts bringing disease, murder, and torture—too much to fathom, declaring he was upsetting the status quo, looking to split the world as they know.

"Finally, there was a third group, who looked upon the words Maarkus shared as a forewarning of death and change. The old chief was one of those. Almost intuitively, he could hear and place the words of truth from those of speculation.

"Maarkus's arrival in a small sailboat with a baby strapped to his back, like a nurturing woman, and a bleating goat, was a sight never seen before and was greeted with laughter as he leapt from the boat stern to haul it onto the bank of the river. The baby was named Ahan in honour of the water god that lived and managed the emerald waters of the green river. Even in the first home, Ahan was recognised as someone special."

Ahan recounted how, as a boy, he grew alongside the chief's son, Amaro, as if they were brothers.

Ahan was nurtured by all the women of the tribe; it was often seen both babes suckling from the same wet nurse, poking fingers at each other. As they grew under the watchful eyes of the women and the wet nurse was replaced with firm foods, the boys were never far apart.

It became difficult for their carers to find Ahan and Amaro in the evenings, as they played anywhere in the grounds and slept in any small resting house they happened to find themselves in.

On many occasions, they were found curled up asleep with a litter of puppies or piglets when they grew too tired to leave.

One day, whilst watching the waves crashing on the shore, Ahan's father, Maarkus, watched in fascination at the differing-sized branches and flotsam making their way on the surface of the waves to float gently to shore. Maarkus tilted his head in curiosity as a ball of excitement bloomed in his stomach. Why not a child or a man? he thought.

It was from here he designed the idea to craft a piece of the lightest wood he could find, large enough to hold a man on top, in this instance his son, Ahan.

Maarkus crafted from his own hand, Ahan's first water board, carefully balancing Ahan, offering gentle encouragement as Ahan began learning the foot pressure and body awareness necessary to control the plank beneath his feet. It wasn't long before Maarkus, his chest bursting with love and pride, watched his only son with three wet seasons of life, gliding smoothly and balancing independently as the waves rolled his son on his board gently into shore.

This skill of wave riding became so popular over that summer season that many of the young men were seen carving their own boards and riding the waves with varying degrees of success. It became such an obsession with the men and women alike, that many necessary hunting and produce gathering tasks were neglected until the elders, who were not attempting the ride, stepped in to reprimand and halt the activity.

#

Ahan's training in medicine and sacred magic began not long after, as young boys' energy and curiosity began to expand in the interest of the people, the wayfarers, were meeting during the many stopovers on the long journey to their new land.

Ahan began his training for knowledge, prompted and bargained for by his father, Maarkus, who first negotiated with the small brown slit-eyed natives on the larger land masses.

The Emerald Water Tribe by this stage were desperate for fresh food and the types of food sources which could be used to stave off the illnesses that drained the travellers of energy, causing swollen, spongy, and purplish gums that were prone to bleeding.

After learning the secrets of the fruits and further sharing of his new knowledge with the other tribes, the travelling wayfarers discovered, Ahan's reputation for the esoteric began to grow.

Ahan was adopted by the fuzzy-headed black island folk who shared their knowledge of the sorcerer's ways of shark hunting in the deep waters of the ocean.

His powers in enticing and hunting these water beasts sustained the wandering sailors in their tribal canoes of many people for countless nights, giving them the necessary fats and nutrients, they needed to survive the long journey on their quest to find their new land.

But it was towards the end of the big journey that Ahan, now a young man, was elevated to the mystical rank of Tohunga that he now held.

For it was Ahan that found the place of the clouds, found them a home, away from the threat of the ghosts, a place of safety, a place of their own.

\#

After many long years at sea, hopping from island to island, bartering for food sources, transferring people from the various islands into the tribe and out, some of the travellers, tired of their quest, chose to stay at the current island the Emerald Water Tribe happened to be visiting.

Ever adaptable the tribe members switched fishing, hunting, and cooking implements for equipment lost at sea, sharing skills and knowledge with island folk as they sailed from one land to another, constantly looking for the terrestrial body that would embrace them as a mother embraces a child. A land that was empty of humans as promised by the ancient ones, ready and waiting for the remnants, the survivors of the Emerald Water Tribe from the old world to embrace.

\#

It was Ahan who had spotted the birds far off on the horizon, feeding on an oceanic corpse that led to the discovery of their new land.

On that wonderful day, Ahan had been experimenting with a cloth that felt as light as air and billowed like a pillow when it caught the breeze.

Ahan bartered hard with the old woman from one of the islands they were visiting for the cloth over many days.

Until, in the end, she ended up with everything he had to offer and had managed to beg from his father.

Ahan attempted to cajole, coerce, and intimidate the old lady into giving him what he wanted.

Unfazed by all his carry-on, the old lady and now a posse of other women sellers, sharing and chewing slowly on pieces of white-fleshed tree fruit, all watched on in amusement at the young man's performance.

#

"Mistress of great beauty," Ahan would begin his rhetoric to the old woman, "You have no need for a cloth of this shabby and poorly made material, I will happily take it off your hands for a generous price of these shells and some delicious, dried fish, guaranteed to sustain your health and prolong your beauty,"

The old woman grunted and Ahan, seeing he had barely made any impression, would continue, "In addition to this generous offer, I have a wonderful cup sculpted in our old world which is said to have magical properties." Ahan leaned in closely as if to impart some secret words. With a backward glance at her friends, the old woman obliged and leaned into the enticing young man to hear what he had to say.

Ahan pulled an unremarkable smooth wooden cup from his satchel. "It was said that any man that drinks from this cup will fall instantly in love and want to place his hot manhood deep into you," Ahan nodded seductively at her.

"And you, most beautiful one—with this cup—could have any man you wished." He winked conspiratorially at her.

In a bevy of laughter from the old woman and her fellow saleswomen, she told him,

"Young man, I have three useless husbands who are only good for servicing me when I want, I do not need any more, and you need to work on your bargaining."

Ahan reluctantly included his jewels from the old land but, in the end, the exchange was sealed with the addition of an exquisitely carved tiny cup with a matching plate made of a shimmering shell that island folk many leagues away had shown them, after a diving expedition in the shallow waters of one of their fresh water atolls.

These particular island folk believed that inside the shell lived the "treasure food of the sea," a disturbing-looking piece of meat that, when eaten, strengthened the body as well as the heart and was a valued treasure given as gifts of luck, prosperity, and peace to those that wore it.

Ahan and his father, Maarkus, had worked on the shells in the bowel of the massive wayfaring watercraft that was his home, grinding night and day; the marine growth and hard white lime shells over the long quiet evenings—when not attending the duties of the watercraft—to finally reveal the glistening inner shell that changed colours in the light.

#

"If I could get more speed by using this wind, I could fly across this water," had been his spirited thought as he carried away his hard-won prize.

He carefully punctured the cloth in the corners, adding a small stiff eyelet of thin bone to stop the sinew from ripping the cloth he had given up so much for.

Grinning in excitement, he quickly tied the cord around his waist through the leather harness rings he had designed to support himself in the pull of the wind and carefully paddling out on his board away from the flotilla.

Looking for the elusive blast of warm air to hit. Ahan did not have to wait long before the winds picked up in a steady stream, with gusts that billowed and tugged at the large cloth, pulling it out of his hands and into the sky.

With a shout of joy, Ahan leaned back on his board, gripping with his knees and feet as he held on to the sinew line, manipulating the wind in his sail. Ahan pumped the cord first one way, then the other, testing the strength and directions the cloth wanted to travel in. As the wind picked up, Ahan began weaving on the top of the water and, with an outburst of "Woohoo," Ahan started a fierce skating across the ocean surface, as the billowing cloth began moving in the force of the wind.

"Would you look at that boy? Where does he come up with the ideas to do that?" exclaimed a woman to another, as Ahan shot past in the distance, water spraying out furiously from the sides of the board.

"Well, he isn't from our tribe, he is a newcomer really," responded a fellow woman watching on.

"He and his father are ghosts, you know, no matter how hard they try to disguise it," stated another, knowingly nodding her head in Ahan's direction.

The small group of women grunted, raising their eyebrows in acknowledgement of the truth behind this statement.

It was this day, that Ahan, out skimming the top of the ocean with his billowing cloth, spotted the tell-tale signs of land.

#

Ahan's reputation grew throughout the tribes over the years, as his exploits were discussed, embellished, and retold, growing larger with each telling until they became legendary.

Of all the legends, the one the tribe folk enjoyed retelling the most was the myth of rebirth and the story of Aõ.

The legend of Ahan's miraculous ability to induce birth by placing—through magical interventions—a child into a barren woman—a demonstration of Ahan's power over life.

Aõ was born to the second most adored wife of the current chief, Amaro.

A miraculous birth to a woman who bore no other children. A child who bore Ahan's eyes and the facial structure of a ghost, demonstrating the proof of his divine intervention.

# Chapter 8

# The Pledge

As Ahan recounted the Emerald Water Tribe's history and his childhood antics to Aõ, the soft lilt of his voice washed over her, luring Aõ back into a restful sleep.

Ahan knew that she would be here in his medicine hut for many long days, healing the organs on the inside before the healing and rehabilitation on the outside—her abilities to walk and move her arms—could begin.

Ahan hung his head in despair; if she was not able to stand straight or contribute to the welfare of the tribe due to disabilities or mental incapacity, there was a very likely chance that the tribe would have her put to death.

A cold anger grew in him as he looked down at her swollen face, her eyes like slits in the swelling of her cheeks. Ahan administered comfrey for the pain in her spine and white willow bark to soothe the swelling. Ahan could see the medicinal concoctions beginning to have an impact but he was still unsure how Aõ would look after the swelling disappeared.

Her nose had been broken and Ahan did his best to reset it.

It would be straighter than what was normal for the tribe's features, where the nose bridge was more flattened with wider nostrils.

Ahan painstakingly built a frame in which her head was ensconced in an effort to have the broken face bones heal as close together as they had once been.

Ahan had done the same for one of Aõ's arms and, again, for one of her legs. It would be a miracle if Aõ could ever run again as she had, thought Ahan.

It was on this thought that Ahan made his silent pledge. Rimachi, a man—young, yes, he is, but still a man—was pitting himself against a helpless girl who had done him no wrong.

A man that could target a girl with such hatred and violence was not chief material; if he could not see the value in diversity, then he is not deserving of the gift of chiefdom. This was the conclusion to the thought stream that flowed through Ahan's mind.

Ahan gently placed his hand on Aõ's chest, as a physician, to feel the rise and fall of her respirations as she slept, and as a spiritual medium to embed his pledge to Aõ.

He removed the small knife he used for cutting herbs and plants.

Ahan found a place between his many sacred tribal markings and dug the tip deep into his chest, making a small adjustment to one of the designs over his heart.

He isolated a small clump of hair from the side of his head, weaving it into an intricate plait, wiping the blood from the knife into the plait before tying off the ends, shearing it from his head. "This is the last time, Aõ, that you will have to suffer at the hands of this man, the spirits and I will work to protect you. Rimachi will never touch you or any other female in such a way again. This is my pledge to you," Ahan tied the plait of hair around Aõ's wrist and gently pulled the covers back up.

Ahan left the room quietly, heading straight out his medicine hut in a direct line to Amaro's, the current chief's house.

## Chapter 9

## Things Are Never as They Seem

Ahan walked quickly, attempting to breathe his anger into nothing—preparing his mind for the conversation he needed to have with his best friend—what was the best way to phrase that his son was a monster?

The guards on either side of the house entrance politely stepped to the middle of the doorway barring Ahan's progress.

"Most Honoured One, you will be allowed to enter once our chief is aware that you wish to see him," stated one of the guards with a respectful head bow.

"Thank you, Kai, I understand, tell me, how is your old lady?" asked Ahan, patiently waiting for the messenger boy to alert Amaro to his presence at the door.

"Her breathing is much easier, thank you, Honoured One, the smoke from the herbs seems to assist with her being able to breathe better—my wife, children, and I are deeply grateful for you and your wisdom," responded Kai. "Her cooking is what keeps me sustained, as much as I love and value my wife, I would starve if it wasn't for our old lady," Kai added in a conspiratorial jest.

Ahan laughed in response. "Yes, our elders do have a way of making food taste extra special."

Ahan stood quietly to one side, waiting patiently, gathering his thoughts as the conversation tapered off between himself and the guards.

What to say and how to phrase the next conversation without offending Amaro and his family was the conversation running through Ahan's mind when the summons to come into Amaro's house was received.

The guards nodded their heads in respect to Ahan as they moved aside to allow him entry.

Nodding back and moving quickly through the open gateway, Ahan made his way across the small compound full of shrubs and decorative plants creatively placed to display a canopy of forest greenery like that of which they had left behind in the old country.

Ahan walked purposefully to the main meeting house, where he knew Amaro would be waiting for him.

As tradition imposed, Ahan entered the main meeting house to make his way to the centre of the room standing with head bowed and hands clasped in front, waiting to be acknowledged by his lifelong friend.

"I see you, my friend, and from your stance I see you are upset about something," stated Amaro as he paced into the room.

Amaro, the Chief of the Emerald Water Tribe, revered from the original lineage of the old country, a traditional Wayfarer of the long journey and pure in blood of the old country, came to stand directly in front of Ahan.

"My friend, the fact that you stand here with so much ceremony tells me the seriousness of the issue you wish to discuss with me," he began. "I believe it is to do with the assault on Aõ allegedly by Rimachi," stated Amaro, waving away his attendants as he moved away from Ahan towards the water pitcher to pour out two cups of herb-infused tea.

Ahan, aware of all the nuances of the words used and the behaviour of his colleague, recognised that his friend was offering a diplomatic platform on which Ahan could discuss his thoughts.

"Yes, my chief," began Ahan. "I am concerned for the girl's safety—she is lucky to survive this assault, Rimachi is pitching himself against a girl who has no choice but to comply. His attack on her was uncalled for," finished Ahan as he took the cup of tea from Amaro.

Amaro sipped his tea in speculation at Ahan's words.

"We do not know for certain that it was Rimachi that caused these injuries," responded Amaro thoughtfully. "All reports suggest she sustained the injuries from the fall," he countered.

Ahan looked up directly at Amaro with contempt across his face at this suggestion.

"I have no doubt, my chief, of the perpetrator of the injuries on Aõ. As a healer, you know I know the differences between injuries from a fall and from those inflicted by another being, be that a person, animal, or bird," he countered.

"I come today to see what we can do to protect our women from him. I fear that his hatred of women will spread and we will begin to see an increase in hurt women and women who will not want to breed for the good of the Green Emerald Water Tribe.

"He is grooming other men to be accepting of beating women and I have seen the disrespectful nature spreading like a sickness amongst his cohorts. It must be stopped now before more assaults occur," finished Ahan.

Amaro, eyes alight with anger. "He is my son and the heir to the chief position of the Emerald Water Tribe," stated Amaro firmly at Ahan.

"Be careful what you say and what you imply," added Amaro as he sat back in his chair, gripping his cup hard as he stared at Ahan.

"I understand, my chief, and Aõ is of my blood, old blood, ancient blood. Rimachi does not need to set himself against a girl that will do as he says it is… " Ahan, lost for words, searched the floor with his eyes and hands outspread and looked for inspiration.

"It is beneath him to do such a thing," Ahan said finally.

He looked directly at Amaro with the meaningful glance that suggested the secret pact they made many years earlier on the wayfaring vessels.

Amaro's look darkened at the unspoken words that lay between them. "Do not look at me like that, like I owe you something. I do not!" he hissed at Ahan.

"You are where you are today because of our friendship, because of me you would have been ostracized from our tribe if it were not for our friendship," added Amaro.

Ahan nodded in agreement to the partial truth of this. "And I will always be grateful for the ancient ones for bringing me to you; to have you as my chief and my friend is a gift," conceded Ahan.

With these soothing words, Amaro took a deep breath, settling back into the knowledge that he still retained the power and control over the medicine man.

Ahan continued, "My chief, it does not change the facts that Aõ was set upon and we need to deal with this unpleasant situation."

"There is no proof that Rimachi was the perpetrator, and until another eyewitness comes forward with visual evidence or something similar, besides Little Big Boy—" he added with derision, "A fourteen-year-old boy who is well known to be prone for exaggerating situations, I may add—I will not be accusing Rimachi of anything except helping you retrieve Aõ from the cliff face," responded Amaro, now disinterested in the conversation.

Amaro, examining his nails and waving towards his stewards for more refreshments, added, "If Aõ does not heal correctly or is found to be barren because of her injuries, there is only one option left for her."

Ahan felt the colour drain from his face and a sense of dread stab in his stomach. He looked up sharply at Amaro "I will not put her to death, my chief, she will still have value no matter how she survives her injuries—if she survives her injuries," he added.

"Well," Amaro said, "You know our traditions, if you remember, you were a part of developing them. We will not carry someone who is unable to contribute to the welfare of the tribe—we are not strong or large enough to support those who drain our resources and will not or cannot enhance us. I will be watching her progress and listening to the reports of her recovery with interest," finished Amaro, turning to the sweet meals that were now being shown to him. And, like that, Ahan was dismissed from his friend's side.

# Chapter 10

# The Search for a Truth

The slow fires of anger and injustice burned deep in Ahan, making him unable to return to the healing hut.

So angered at his friend's naivety, too inflamed with rage at his friend, Amaro's denials to see the truth, and that Amaro chose to pitch a threat towards Aõ.

If he tried to work against Rimachi, Amaro would find some fault in Aõ's recovery and Aõ would effectively be sentenced to death.

Ahan wanted to smash something, to feel the breaking or crush or anything in his hands.

He clenched his fists, breathing hard through his nostrils, willing for calm so he could think of a strategy to salvage the impending situation. His firm stomping made people nearby scramble out of his way, wide-eyed at what could have upset the medicine man so much.

He strode towards the front gates, down the long path to circle in behind the compound. When he arrived at the bottom of the hill, he peered carefully up at the cliff face. Ahan began to see the signs of the treacherous path that wove its zigzag way up the side to disappear between some poorly maintained fencing.

"Why was she coming and going via this route?" wondered Ahan. "What was she doing, what was she hiding?"

Ahan began the climb up the cliff face. Carefully placing his feet and hands, he made good progress, but still arrived breathless where they found Aõ lying in a pool of her own blood.

As he stopped to catch his breath, he looked around carefully at the area, noting every twisted or distorted blade of grass and branch, spotting an object out of place, hidden in the grass.

Ahan approached the object slowly, mindful not to disturb the environment in case it changed the picture laid out before him. Squatting down nearby, to examine it before daring to touch it. It was a reasonably designed tool, simple in nature but designed for throwing things—stones, Ahan surmised, a hunting weapon. Ahan nodded to himself at the rationale of this as he reached out to take the object, turning the item over, examining it from all angles. "Cleverly made," he decided as he gave it a swing. Designed to enhance the power of the thrower and effective, no doubt, for bringing down small prey. So now he had a reason for why Aõ was using this track – she was breaking tradition and hunting with a man's weapon she had designed herself, concluded Ahan with a shake of his head, muttering obscenities under his breath. Ahan hunted around the area for a short time, noting the footprints of the men that had assisted with retrieving Aõ, finding Aõ's dried blood spots on the ground and grass. Ahan bent down, withdrawing his herb knife to cut the grass crusted with blood. Carefully tying the bundle of grass together, he stashed it in his satchel.

Noting nothing else of value, Ahan began tracking with his eyes the route back down the cliff face before making the descent to the ground.

When he finally stepped on solid ground, Ahan began scanning the ground for the tell-tale signs of footprints and subtly broken grass stems and bent branches indicating the path that Aõ had taken into the forest.

# Chapter 11

# Pathways and Eggs

Ahan walked quietly, retracing Aõ's trek through the forest. Ahan could see, as he made his way around trees, the familiar tracks made by the hunter, those made by the women as they foraged for greens, and the small tracks left by animals on the hunt for even smaller prey.

The track Aõ had taken was a long meander through the thicker, more impenetrable sections of the forest. To avoid detection, thought Ahan as he leapt over fallen branches, placing his feet carefully where the disturbed moss on fallen branches indicated Aõ had placed her feet when she had moved through.

The track was newly formed, the ground still covered in damp leaf litter, low-lying branches hung across the path blocking the view in front. Ahan pushed these aside, his eyes flicking to the ground to search for the small signs of disturbance to indicate the path Aõ had taken.

Ahan circled around a large tree to stop suddenly as a clearing opened up before him. Ahan, surprised by the suddenness of the clearing, ducked down to hide his presence and breathe in deeply at the beauty of nature around him.

The trees had just stopped, opening to a sun-kissed field that still shimmered with the late afternoon mist slowly rising into the warming air.

It was perhaps the most singular beautiful place he had encountered in this wondrous land of no enemy.

"The ancients truly spoke the truth when they indicated there was a land that was pure, untouched by man, inhabited with beasts and resources ready for the man that could take them, a tribe that was worthy of the austerity of this land," marvelled Ahan at the sight before him.

Ahan settled down beneath a fallen log to ascertain the layout of the land—the animals that fed and made this oasis their ground. It was no surprise to him that the oversized megafauna of Moa made an immediate appearance in their small-in-number but large-in-size flocks. Wary of their aggressive nature, he settled in beneath the log to study their behaviours. I wonder how often Aõ has been here watching these amazing creatures, thought Ahan as he studied the Moas' mannerisms towards each other. As he watched intensely, Ahan began to recognise the patterns of nurture. He observed in the distance how the larger black Moas gently herded the smaller ones together to keep them in a group. Ahan smiled to himself at this sight.

Like how our older and breeding women care for the youngest, he surmised with a smile.

Look at how that Moa smacks its beak against the smaller Moa to push it in another direction to feed, thought Ahan, fascinated by the exchange occurring in front of him by the very beasts that slaughtered the men of the Emerald Water Tribe.

He began making his way cautiously and quietly around the outskirts of the field.

Ahan, with eyes still focused intensely on the feeding flock, found himself pressed against the rock face. With a quick look behind, he could see the opening to a cave hidden behind hanging branches which worked as a screen obscuring the entry.

Moving sideways with a fluid motion, he slipped into a hidden recess.

Surprised at where he found himself, Ahan shifted his view to the space he found himself in.

Sheltered and secure from the elements, Ahan peered around; off to one side was a pile of the most oversized objects he had ever seen.

Ahan cautiously made his way over to the precariously made nest of thin branches and sand scraped into a semicircle of protection. There, in the centre of the nest, were three oversized, yellow-tinged eggs.

#

Ahan squatted down next to them , tentatively placing a hand on the topmost egg to determine its warmth and viability. Ahan closed his eyes, willing the ancient one to give him some insight about the current situation he found himself in—to contemplate his next move.

With a smile, he cradled the topmost egg and gently slid it into his satchel.

As cautious as ever, Ahan made his way out of the sandy cave, edging quietly around the outer edges of the field filled with grazing Moa, Ahan discreetly began his pathway back to the healing hut.

# Chapter 12

# Growth and Life

"Aõ, are you awake?" asked Ahan as he slipped into the medicine hut that evening.

Aõ stirred, shaking her head from side to side, attempting to move off the herb-induced coma Ahan had prescribed his acolytes to give her.

"'I have a gift for you," he said as he watched Aõ stir from the depths of sleep.

"A gift?" Aõ murmured..

Ahan presented the oversized egg to her.

"The ancient ones have seen fit to put in my path a potential offspring of the Moa.

"I do not have the capacity or desire to care for such a thing. You, on the other hand, as a child of the Emerald River—being incapacitated—will have the time and, eventually, the energy to teach an offspring of this egg the ways of the Emerald Water Tribe, IF you decide to live and IF it decides to live. What say, you, Aõ of the Emerald Water Tribe? Will you accept this token of life to nurture?

"You must keep it warm; you must turn it slightly every day; if it is viable, it will hatch. You must be the first thing the chick sees when it emerges from the shell. Do you understand, Aõ?" asked Ahan.

"I understand, Ahan, thank you but I don't know how I can do this when I can't move," said Aõ, perplexed at this strange obligation she agreed to.

"By the time this chick is ready to move, you will have to be also," he said with an encouraging nod.

"These things are not to be considered yet; the first thing you must do is keep this egg warm. The shell is thick, you will not break it with the small movements you can make at the moment. Be sure to remind the carers when they come to assist you that you are now the carer of this egg." Ahan tucked the egg in snugly next to Aõ and prepared to leave. With a final glance at her, Ahan left the small room.

#

The days bled into each other for Aõ. Much of Aõ's time, though, was spent in long periods of medicinal sleep. With the assistance of the acolytes, she would be woken briefly to eat soft food, drink the special healing tonics, and to attend to her ablutions. Slowly, Aõ's body began to mend.

Aõ's drug-induced coma meant she missed the regular visitors that came by on a daily basis to sit with her. Most days, Warea would be sitting by her bed, pulling out her current weaving or woodwork activity, beginning her work quietly.

On this particular day, the curtain was pulled back abruptly as Little Big Boy stepped through.

"Good morning, my Lady," he said respectfully, bowing his head to Warea, who responded with a nod.

"And a good morning to you, Maka, you are late this morning," noted Warea as she began stripping the fibres from the Flax fronds.

Maka—Little Big Boy—dragged a stool across the room to sit next to Warea.

"They made me herd the pigs out to the field at daybreak, there was one pig that would not follow, and this pig kept going in the opposite direction to the other pigs! I do not understand why it would not stay with the others, I spent all morning chasing it down," replied an exasperated Little Big boy as he reached out to grab a frond and began helping Warea strip back the flesh to expose the fibres.

"I prefer this type of task, Warea, to running around in the mud like a maniac," he added as he expertly worked the fibres to a soft texture.

Warea nodded her head in amusement. Little Big Boy did suit more of the women's tasks and had already produced some excellent garments and ornamental urns from turned wood, she thought to herself.

"Yes, Maka, there is always one in every group that is different from the rest of the herd. But that does not mean that he is any less than the others, only that he thinks differently and his needs are different," responded Warea.

"We are all different—it is like the tree which needs to grow, the tree that is in the richer soil may grow bigger and stronger than the tree next to it. But the small tree, which has fought harder to grow, will last longer when the men come to choose which tree will be used for the next water raft or fence post.

"Men will always choose the bigger trees for their immediate needs, for its sturdiness and strength and that will be the tree that's cut down first.

"But what will endure will be the smaller tree, dismissed by men for its lack of growth, for its lack of strength. Men will remember the part of the forest that the small tree grew in, for its lack of growth. However, one day, that small tree will be the biggest in girth and strength, Nothing is always as it seems," said Warea, nodding at her statement as she reached into her pocket to pull out some small, coloured stones.

She raised her eyebrows in a questioning manner at Little Big Boy, hoping that he understood her conversational nuances.

"Will you join us in a game today? The other ladies will be here soon. I like that necklace with the tiny polished wooden beads you made, I would be happy to take them off your hands in the games today," she stated with a smile.

Little Big Boy grinned back at her. "And I like your bracelet with the white gems; I would be very happy for you to put them forward as a prize also," he retorted as he added the fibrous strands to the growing pile in front of them.

Warea and Little Big Boy smiled at each other in comfortable comradery as they continued quietly in working through their task.

"Aõ-aho," a voice called out softly as a small group of elder women made their way into the now cramped bedroom space.

"Did you remember the gaming pieces?" asked a wizened old lady at Warea, who nodded as she placed a cushion down on a stool for the old lady to sit next to Little Big Boy. The old lady gave Little Big Boy a gentle tap on the hand and peered at him through her wrinkled face. "Do I know you?" she asked suspiciously.

"Yes, my lady, I am Maka, your brother, Ahe-Ahe's grandson," replied Little Big Boy tapping her hand back in affection, fully aware of the routine they went through every time she saw him.

"Ahhhhhh, yes, I remember now, Maka. Yes, Maka." She nodded to herself. "Have I seen Maka?" she asked confusingly at Little Big Boy.

Little Big Boy rolled his eyes in exasperation at her forgetfulness. "Yes, my lady, I am Maka," he responded, tapping his chest to indicate his name.

In an attempt to change the subject, Little Big Boy asked, "Did you bring something to play with, my lady?"

The old lady tapped the side of her nose and peered gleefully at him through her numerous wrinkles, her eyes like bright black buttons. She pulled from under her cloak an exquisite necklace made of pearls. "I have these," she whispered.

Little Big Boy gasped in pleasure, clutching his hands together with eyes wide open at the splendour of the necklace. At the unveiling of such exquisite jewellery, they were quickly swamped by the other women. In excitement, they cleared away a table and began their gambling, eager to get their hands, if only for a moment, on the riches being offered up for prizes in the day's gambling.

Aõ stirred in her delirium and awoke sleepily to the crackling of laughter of wins and exclamation of losses as the budgets of the players moved from one player to the other.

Aõ lay there, listening to the sweet sounds of fun, feeling rested and at ease; something she had not felt in a long time. She cradled the egg, moving it gently to another side to ensure that each section got a good degree of warmth.

"I see you, my friend," she whispered to the egg, in amongst all the noise. "I wonder what you will be like. I wonder how tall you will be. I am excited to meet you. I hope you will want me as a friend," she murmured with warmth in her heart to the egg.

Warea, hearing the gentle murmurs, looked back at Aõ.

Seeing her awake, she quickly left her chair at the game to come to the bedside to gently stroke the side of Aõ's face, planting a gentle, loving kiss on her forehead.

"I see you are awake; you are looking much better today," she said gently to Aõ, stroking her face and hair with a smile of love on her face.

"Yes, Warea, I feel much better, I am very happy to see you and all the elder women here; I did not know they were coming to visit me," said Aõ.

Warea hummed at this. "Well, my lovely, it is because they wanted to check on your progress as well as see each other in a safe place," she tapered off with a sly smile.

Aõ looked back at Warea with a grin.

"What you mean is there is no other place to play stones so you have all come here under the guise of visiting me?" Aõ and Warea grinned at each other.

Warea responded, "We have been coming here every week, sometimes twice a week to 'visit'; we have all enjoyed coming and seeing how strong you are getting. You have been doing a good job with looking after that egg, too."

"I hope it hatches for you; we have already decided that if it were not to be, the elders would be very respectful and ensure that we add lots of spices when we cook up the foetus—you may even get some of the first portion after the chief," offered Warea.

Aõ, hugging her egg tighter to her body, swallowed in distaste at the thought of eating her substitute baby.

"Thank you—I am honoured," she replied. "But I am sure this egg will hatch."

#

The game of stones continued for some time, until the caregivers, who had turned a blind eye to the shenanigans of the old ladies, came in to feed and assist Aõ with her ablutions.

"Stay, Little Big Boy, will you help me?" asked Aõ, as the caregivers shooed the elders out and began setting Aõ's meal items out.

"I would be honoured, my friend," he responded, relieving the caregiver of the meal and spoon, eyes gleaming at the delicious soft choicest meats, gravy, and vegetables piled in the corner of the bowl.

The caregiver nodded, with a verbal warning to Little Big Boy not to eat Aõ's food and, with a final hard eyeballing at him, she left to attend to other tasks.

Immediately, Little Big Boy popped a mouthful of food in his mouth. "Mmmmm, this is delicious, if bodily injuries didn't hurt so much, I would love to be here being waited on hand and foot," he murmured through his food.

Aõ grinned as Little Big Boy put the food down and propped Aõ up higher in the bed. He began alternating spoonfuls of food between Aõ and himself.

It wasn't long before their quiet mastication was interrupted by a flurry of activity and voices on the other side of the divider.

"Quickly, bring her in here, how long has Leani been bleeding?" Aõ recognised the voice of Mara asking questions of those bringing a woman into the room next door.

"I do not know. She never said anything. Leani just collapsed onto the floor of the hut and that was when I noticed the blood," replied the scared voice of an older woman.

"Do not worry, I will give her something to stop the bleeding—hopefully. Ahan is out seeing other people but a messenger will find him soon and he will be back to look at her," replied Mara as she shoved towels under the girl and propped her hips up on the bed.

"What happened to you?" Mara asked the girl Leani.

Aõ and Little Big Boy leaned in closer to the divider, eyes wide, listening intently to the conversation next door.

Aõ and Little Big Boy looked at each other, as no response came from the girl on the other side of the divider.

"Do not hide what happened—we cannot treat you correctly if you do not tell us how this came about," encouraged Mara. "Did you feel sick? Is it the time of your flow and it hasn't stopped?

"Are you experiencing trouble breathing or pain here?" asked Mara.

Aõ and Little Big Boy heard the girl gasp and cry out in pain as Mara pressed down on a section of the girl's abdomen.

The two eavesdroppers heard Mara order the older woman to leave.

When the older woman left, Mara began her line of urgent questioning again.

"Leani, you must tell me what happened, from the hardness and shape of your belly, I suspect there is a baby in you and the baby is not well, and this is why you are bleeding," said Mara.

Aõ and Little Big Boy's eyes went wide; they looked at each other and turned their heads back to the divider.

A gentle sobbing began, gaining in strength until it became a great rush of breath and emotional outpouring.

"It was not what I wanted, they did not give me a choice, Mara, they held me down, and I did not want this," the girl sobbed. "And now there will be a baby and no father to help me care for it; I do not know what to do."

"Leani, what do you mean, they held you down? Who held you down and did this to you?" asked Mara, her eyes widened in alarm as she sucked her breath in dismay at what Leani was implying.

Aõ and Little Big Boy did not hear the response, but, looking at each other intuitively, guessing who the perpetrators would have been.

Little Big Boy clutched at Aõ's hand in solidarity of their thoughts.

"You are not the only one, Aõ," he whispered, leaning in close to her. "Leani has been hurt by Fat Knuckles and his group too from the sounds of things."

Aõ whispered back, "We do not know this for sure; it could be anyone."

Little Big Boy shrugged with indifference. "I bet my new pearly necklace it was him and his cronies," he retorted.

He sighed in defeat. "I have to go anyway; there are some pigs in the back field waiting for my delightful presence to bring them in," replied Little Big Boy, flourishing his arms about in a dramatic fashion.

Aõ nodded, smiling at him. "Yes, go, my friend, I am so happy to have seen you, thank you for today," she replied.

Little Big Boy gave her a gentle kiss on the forehead. "You will be ugly and maimed when you come out of here—but I will still be your friend," he said with a wink as he pulled back the dividing curtain and, with a flapping hand wave, he disappeared out of sight.

Aõ's smiles turned to surprise as she heard him exclaim in disgust, "Eeuh, there's blood all over the ground, I almost slipped in it, do you have any idea how long it took me to make this shirt? I would never get the blood stains out if I would have fallen," he projected angrily at the caregiver helping Leani as he edged carefully around the pool of blood on the floor.

"Go away, you stupid-looking goat's arse," was the hostile response Aõ heard to Little Big Boy's retort about his shirt. "The words coming out of your mouth are like the piss spraying from a pig's hole, you ridiculous little half man."

Aõ cringed in her bed at the onslaught Little Big Boy was receiving from Leani's attendant.

"That's right, keep walking, shithead," was the last call the attendant made at Little Big Boy, before turning her attention back to her patient.

For the rest of that evening and the weeks that followed, Aõ found herself being pushed down the priority list, as more women began filtering in the door of the healing hut with a myriad of physical injuries.

Aõ, unable to see and only able to hear, caught the snippets of conversation drifting through the dividing curtain.

Aõ, understanding the breach of privacy, couldn't help attempting to garner as much information as she could get, to build the suspicions that Little Big Boy had voiced about Fat Knuckles.

It was one random morning, as the caregiver helped Aõ to wash, Aõ boldly asked outright,

"Mara, I could not help but overhear; there seems to be a lot of women coming into the healing huts with physical injuries. I am sorry, I do not mean to eavesdrop, but it is hard not to hear."

Mara nodded as she drew the washcloth gently down Aõ's back. "Yes, it is. I hope the noises do not disturb you too much, Ahan would be very upset if you were to become unwell and all the healing we have achieved has been undone."

Aõ nodded her head in understanding. "You do not need to worry, or let Ahan know anything except I am healing well," she responded. "It is just that I am curious about their injuries. What do you think is happening, Mara?"

Mara nodded and grunted in acknowledgement. She gently rolled Aõ onto her side to begin washing the back of her legs.

"It seems that you are not the only one with lies," she began, looking knowingly at Aõ.

Aõ blushed at this comment, reflecting back over the weeks, to the questioning Mara conducted with her when she had first awoken after being attacked by Fat Knuckles.

Mara nodded her head. "Not one of the women is saying anything; it is frustrating and I suspect it is fear that is holding their tongues still," stated Mara,

"Ahan sees it; I suspect he knew of it before the women's injuries started. I am not sure why he has not been able to prevent it from happening. It must be a magic that he is unfamiliar with."

Mara tilted her head in interest at Aõ. "Is there something you are seeing, Aõ?" asked Mara.

Aõ, eyes widened in innocence, shook her head emphatically in denial.

#

Leani rolled over onto her side in an attempt to get comfortable.

She looked at the concoction Ahan had given to her mother with strict instructions to have Leani drink it once in the morning and evening, to aid in strengthening her womb and improve the clotting factors of her blood.

Not so long ago, Leani had been tending to chores, learning the new traditional tunes and dance movements to enhance the songs, helping with the minor preparation of cooking and weaving as befitting for a girl of fourteen years.

Then, her world had been turned inside out.

The early signs of warming weather inspired Leani to forage in the lower fields outside the compound. There, in the wetter sections of the open expanse, grew a water-loving plant with sweet tender shoots she knew her old lady would enjoy for her evening meal.

Leani had been humming quietly to herself when she heard the snap of twigs nearby.

She straightened in fright at the sound, to find herself surrounded by a group of young men.

Naive to the very start of the assault, Leani smiled and nodded her head in friendship towards them.

"Good morning, there are some delicious shoots awake now and ready for picking," she began gesturing to the water plants. "Shut your face," was the response she got. Surprised at the abrasiveness and hostility of Rimachi's response, Leani blinked and began talking again.

"I am sorry, Rimachi, I did not mean to offend you in any way, and I am happy for you to share what I have picked," she replied, holding the bowl of shoots out.

Rimachi smashed his hand down on the bowl, spilling the entire contents onto the ground.

"You are pretty but very stupid," he said menacingly. "You should not be out of the compound. You are a woman; do you not know the kinds of things that can happen to a young woman when you are not under the protection of your chief and within the confines of the compound?" he countered back at her, distaste in the form of a sneer stamped across his face.

"But, I am a woman of the Emerald Water Tribe on Emerald Water grounds, I do not have anything to be concerned about," countered Leani, hands held wide in confusion at his hostile reception.

The young man turned to his cohorts with a crooked smile on his face as he eyeballed each of them, and then responded to the girl's answer,

"That is a mistake, faulty thinking that many women make, assuming you are protected because you are a woman of the Emerald Water Tribe. It is not so; you have to earn your place in this tribe if you are to stay."

With a slight nod of his head, two men stepped forward to take hold of Leani's arms, forcing her onto her knees and then face down to the ground.

#

Leani, lying on her side in the corner of her mother's hut, shut her eyes, and pressed her hands over her ears in an attempt to shut out the memories and sounds of how she came to be in her predicament. She was now with child, but unsure who the father of the child was. The child would become a child of the tribe, growing up on whatever kindness a tribe member had to offer, being passed around amongst the tribe seeking food and shelter because she was without a man to help. Her mother, still unknowing of her state, would know soon enough and demand Leani tell her how it happened.

It had been hard enough for her mother to live off the generosity of the tribe when Leani's father had been killed in a hunting mishap some years earlier. It had been his stoic reputation and skills as a hunter which allowed them to continue living in comfort and be offered good quality samples of the food that was brought in by the various hunting parties and plant foragers.

There was enough for the two of them to survive but the generosity only extended as far as the hunter's wife and immediate offspring.

The next generation was expected to fend for themselves and contribute to the overall gathering and sharing of the entire tribe. Without a partner to assist in this task as her pregnancy progressed, she would be left with the least nutritious meat, and vegetables that were only fit for the animals to consume.

Leani was young, touched by another man, men really, and without a partner. Her prospects of a happy outcome of love and partnership were not high.

Unless, Leani thought, she approached the parents of the man whom she knew definitively was there, she might yet save the face of both her and her mother. Leani contemplated this thought throughout the night.

#

The next morning, Leani woke and made her way gingerly to the ablution area. Her stomach still cramped in an uncomfortable manner as she walked down to the women's area to urinate. She pulled down the small, padded undergarment that had been fashioned for women to wear when their moon courses happened. As she bent down to squat, she noted the brownish blood staining on the soft pad that lined the undergarment. It appeared that the bleeding had almost stopped and there was no stinging when she passed her urine.

Leani nodded in acceptance of this, unsure if she should be happy or concerned about this development.

She made her way to the river shore, stripping her clothes off.

Leani stooped down to soak her washing clothes in the cold water of the river and noted the slight swelling of her abdomen now starting to protrude.

As she ran the cold wet cloths over her body, her emotions were mixed with brief ecstatic happiness that she was with child, to the overwhelming sadness of how the child came to be.

The visit to the healing hut scared her far more than she had thought and it was at the point when she realised she might lose the baby, that had cemented in her heart that she would have this baby regardless of the outcome.

Despite her resolution, her vanity was still thankful for the long cloak that would hide her pregnancy until it was time to give birth.

Leani washed herself vigorously, making her skin tingle with the energetic scrubbing. She felt energised, ready to tackle whatever came her way. She brushed out her hair carefully, curling the ends to ensure they fell seductively over her right shoulder in a soft wave; with a final scrubbing out of her mouth with a mint-flavoured twig, she made her way back to her mother's hut.

Leani made her decision.

She put on her best skirt and top, smoothing down the decorative beads that adorned the neckline of the shirt. She carefully applied the dark coal eyeliner to enhance the almond shape and draped her hair elegantly over one shoulder.

Taking a deep breath to gather her inner strength, Leani began walking towards the chief's house. As she walked across the compound, she held her head high, determined to ignore the group of young men gathered around the corner of a hut that they used as their place of relaxation. The young men began nudging each other as they spotted Leani walking slowly across the grassy open area.

Instinctively, Leani stopped in her tracks, her hand unwittingly moving to touch the small bulge of her stomach.

Amongst the men hanging in the front of the hut was Rimachi, leaning on one of the carved poles of the hut. He tilted his head in interest at her hand movement.

A few seconds later, indicating with hand signals beckoning the men in, he leaned over to whisper conspiratorially to the other young men who crowded so closely to hear what he had to say.

#

Leani began to breathe heavily as the nervousness of this situation unfolded before her.

She did not want to walk pass the men's hut, but it was deliberately placed directly in front of the main entrance to the chief's compound.

For one to get to the gate of the chief's residence, one had to walk past this hut.

Leani did not have a choice.

Tears began to well in the corner of Leani's eyes as her anxiety escalated with each step.

She picked up her walking pace, refusing to look in the direction of the men's hut.

Her eyes were directed to the entrance of the chief's residence. Three of the men hanging around the men's hut ran out to block her progress, whilst Rimachi continued to lean on the post, examining his fingernails, watching on with a detached face.

"Leani, you are looking very beautiful today, where are you going?" asked one young man called Aleki, a thick-set male in both arm and torso, placing his hand on her arm.

Leani jerked her arm away. "Do not touch me, Aleki!" she exclaimed angrily at him.

"None of you touch me!" she stated firmly, looking at the three men first, then towards those men lounging at the entrance to the men's hut. "I am going to see the chief; there are some things I need to talk to him about."

"What could be so important that someone like you, who is nothing, needs to see the chief?" asked another young man in a joking manner.

Leani looked at him surprised at his nasty comment.

"That is none of your business, Liosi, and you and I are from the same status, by the way," Leani interjected at him. Leani moved around the men and began to quickly walk away, head held high, with a small, satisfied feeling at standing up for herself.

Leani, with her eyes glued to the inner compound gates, almost made it without mishap.

If she had just looked down to check where she was stepping she may have seen Liosi's muscular tattooed leg outstretched to trip her up.

If she slowed down her haste, she would have been able to feel Aleki's hand on her back as he held her still for a minute to plunge a sharp thin needle-like stone that pierced through the soft leather cloak to be driven up under her ribs. Leani, with a push from Aleki, fell hard to the ground on her stomach in a scream of surprise and pain.

#

The door of the healing hut was flung open wildly as Liosi, the young man who had tripped Leani, entered.

Leani lay in his arms, her eyes clenched shut, shallow breathing in groans of agony, hands clasped between her legs attempting to halt the pain and dripping blood.

Leani was semi-unconscious with pain and injury from two sources.

"What happened?" asked the caregiver in incredulity as he pointed to the treatment table for the man to lay Leani down. "I am not sure what has happened," replied Liosi. "She was walking across the compound, I was talking to her, and she then went to continue on her way. I saw Leani clutch her stomach and then she fell over." He replied holding his bloodied hands up, feigning ignorance.

"Someone must get Ahan to return now," replied the caregiver, "And find Leani's mother too," he ordered. Shooing the hovering elder women helping for the day, and Liosi, out of the hut in earnest.

In the room next door, Aõ could hear all the commotion.

Leani is back again. Being carried in the arms of Liosi, one of Rimachi's henchmen? thought Aõ suspiciously. I wonder what Little Big Boy would say about that? she concluded.

The noise in the room next door died down as Leani groaned loudly in agony as the caregiver attempted to get a coherent response from her.

Aõ, in her bed next door, clutching at her egg and blankets, listened anxiously, willing the girl to give some indication of her injuries.

Leani gave no response as she lay there writhing in agony.

Abruptly, Ahan burst into the room, flinging his medicine bag down on the preparation table.

"I know what has happened from the recount of elders," he began as he washed his hands and instructed the caregivers to strip back Leani's clothing to begin his assessment.

"I will assume it is from the fall, injuring the organ holding her babe; that is the primary cause of her bleeding and pain?" he began as he started looking at Leani from the face working his eyes down to ascertain any other abnormalities in her presentation.

The caregiver confirmed Ahan's statement, began voicing his additional findings since Leani arrived.

Ahan interrupted his story with a raised hand gesture. "What is this?" he murmured in surprise, leaning in closer, running his finger over the small stone that appeared to be lodged just under her lower left rib.

"It is nothing, Honoured One, a small stone splinter she obtained when she fell maybe, but nothing that would induce the bleeding to this extent," answered the caregiver.

"We will have to retrieve that later," replied Ahan as he nodded at the caregiver's response to his questioning and dismissed it.

"We need to stop her bleeding as a first priority or she and this baby will die."

Aõ, in the next room, divided only by the flimsy beaded curtain, clutched at the blanket and her egg, pulling it in closer in anxiety for the poor girl on the table in the next room.

As the night progressed, Leani's mother sat silently in a chair, watching the caregivers working in earnest, mixing potions and tonics, salves and herbal compress applicants for the dying girl writhing in unconscious pain.

Aõ was no longer the primary concern, as the caregivers fought to save the girl in front of them.

Aõ, half asleep, heard the final orders of Ahan in the early hours of the morning.

"The baby needs to be delivered now, or she will not survive," came Ahan's final decision as attempt after attempt of life-saving techniques failed to stem the flow of blood or pull the girl from her unconscious pain state.

Aõ could hear Leani begin coughing and vomiting and a high-pitched squeal began emanating from the unconscious girl.

"What is happening, Ahan, I am confused, why is she vomiting blood?" Aõ heard one of the caregivers ask in a perplexed manner.

"She has another injury that has occurred internally," he replied. "That is the only explanation for her ongoing presentation."

"Did we do something to her?" the caregiver voiced in horror at the thought of their treatments causing additional harm to an already dying girl.

"I do not think so; Leani has a strange injury under her rib which I chose not to address at the time, as I was more concerned at the bleeding, but maybe I should have looked into it more deeply," replied a fatigued Ahan.

Towards the early morning, Leani slipped into death. Aõ was awoken by the high-pitched wailing of distress that began from both Leani's mother and the exhausted caregivers.

Leani gave birth to a tiny stillborn male foetus and died shortly after. She never regained consciousness.

#

Aõ, lost in her own trauma of what she had heard, what she experienced as a listener to the intense suffering of pain and final death of the girl in the room next to her, left a profound sense of loneliness in Aõ.

In an almost desperate attempt to nurture life, the cultivation of the large egg tucked under Aõ's arm or between her legs and the responsibility of keeping it warm, turning it regularly, gave Aõ a purpose to focus on whilst the grieving process for the death of an Emerald Water Tribe member progressed.

The caregivers, distracted in their grief for the loss of Leani and her baby, and their sense of helplessness at what had appeared on the surface, a patient they should have been able to save, if not keep pain-free, began to neglect their regular duties of caring for Aõ as stipulated by Ahan.

#

A couple of days later, Little Big Boy and Warea were allowed to visit Aõ.

"You must help me get out of here," demanded Aõ as Little Big Boy and Warea pushed back the divider and walked into her bed space.

"I cannot stand it in here!" she added with tears rolling down her face.

Aõ recounted the entire story as she knew it, including her suspicions of Leosi's involvement in Leani's fall.

Little Big Boy and Warea looked gravely at each other, nodding their heads in sympathy, as Warea gently gathered Aõ in her arms for comfort.

"I am so sorry that you heard all that, my precious one," began Warea. "Ahan, his caregivers, and the elder group have been kept extremely busy these last few days."

Aõ, soothed in the hug by her caregiver and by the presence of her best friend, asked, "What has been happening, Warea?"

Both Little Big Boy and Warea breathed deeply, and, as Warea began to speak, Little Big Boy, unable to contain himself, interrupted Warea before she could get a word out.

"Well.," began Little Big Boy, "You would not believe the events that have been escalating around the tribe, Aõ," he began with a flourish of his hands. Warea sat back in resignation, happy to let Little Big Boy recount the events of the last few weeks whilst Aõ had been recovering.

"When the men went out hunting a couple of days back, two boys, not from our tribe but from the Bush Tribe to the east, were found mutilated and, when I say mutilated, I mean hung upside down, drained of blood with their guts pulled out which were used to tie their hands together. That is not the work of an animal but that of a man, or men," he added tapping the side of his nose in a knowing way. "A brutal way to find death," he added, pushing his haphazard braids back behind his shoulders.

Aõ looked at Warea for confirmation. Warea nodded slowly in agreement. "It is the truth, Aõ. It has caused such anger and blame between the Emerald Water Tribe and the Bush Tribe; they were found just outside the hunting grounds on the boundaries of our lands and theirs. They should not have been on our side but this is no way for them to be punished. The Bush Tribe believe the Emerald Water Tribe is responsible for their deaths but there is no proof. No one is stepping up to acknowledge even seeing the boys at all, therefore, the blame appears unfounded. Chief Amaro is putting a delegation together to go see the Bush chief, and Amaro and Ahan are both going."

"There is more terrible news," added Little Big Boy to Warea's statements.

"Chief Amaro is leaving the welfare of The Emerald Water Tribe to Rimachi while he is away," he stated with wide eyes, nodding to confirm the seriousness of this statement.

This is bad news, thought Aõ. I'm a sitting target here without the protection of Ahan.

"You must get me up and help me to start walking, Little Big Boy," said Aõ. "Rimachi knows exactly where I am and I will be as dead as Leani if I stay here without Ahan's protection."

## Chapter 13

## The Big Bird

It was that evening that Aõ was woken by the gentle rocking movement of the giant egg tucked warmly in the crook of her arm.

Aõ called out to the caregiver in excitement, "It's happening!"

Tonight's caregiver was called Ani, an older rotund woman, who came, blinking sleep from her face, bustling into the room anxious that something happened to her ward.

"I felt the egg moving!" exclaimed Aõ, peering at the now still egg lying in the crook of her arm.

Ani was not amused by the nighttime waking, grunting back at Aõ, "When your chick has arrived, let me know then. This birthing could take all night and there is little we can do to help the chick. Best to let it make its own way into this world, as nature intended." She petted Aõ's arm and she sleepily made her way out of the small room. As an afterthought, she added, "It is my understanding that, in the morning, you wish to try to walk. So said that little busybody friend of yours?"

"Yes, Ani," responded Aõ. "It is time for me to try my legs and arms properly. And if this chick survives the next few hours, I will need to be able to forage and find food for it," Aõ replied as she watched Ani, already falling back into sleep, making her way back to bed.

All through the early hours of the morning, Aõ watched her chick emerging from the amniotic casing it had been growing in for the last eight weeks in her care.

By morning, an exhausted Aõ had her chick. The bird was bigger than any other chicks Aõ had ever seen. The soft down of the bird was still damp and flattened against its large pink, wrinkled body. Aõ softly twilled a whistle at the chick. It turned its head towards the sound, eyes bulging beneath its closed eyelids, which began to slowly attempt to blink in response to Aõ's twills, its soft transparent beak opening in an attempt to squawk.

Aõ stroked the wobbling head of the chick, gently touching the body and wings in marvel at how a creature can come from such an object. as she touched the body, the eyes of the chick, stimulated by the feel, opened to peer drunkenly at Aõ.

#

That morning, as arranged, Little Big Boy turned up to help Aõ out of bed.

Aõ, sitting on the edge, leg stuck out in front thanks to the casing still around it, held her chick wrapped in a soft blanket of fur up for Little Big Boy to see.

"It hatched overnight, Little Big Boy. I'm a mother," she smiled excitedly.

Little Big Boy shivered in thinly veiled disgust at the ugly oversized chick Aõ held in front of him. "Hmm, well, I can see it has your looks," he jokingly commented.

As Aõ pushed the chick in his direction, Little Big Boy flinched away. "No, I do not want to touch that... beauty," he stated, physically pulling away with his hand outstretching in a display of un-welcomeness.

#

Aõ's first tentative steps showed how weak she had become whilst recovering. More worrying was the left leg that was broken, Aõ could not bear on it at all. It was smaller than the other leg and the muscle wastage to the limb was significantly more obvious.

Little Big Boy ticked his tongue against his lips. "This is not good, Aõ."

Ani, also in attendance, added her analysis of the situation.

"Thanks to the bracing Ahan placed on your leg, your limb appears straight but that does not mean that the limb has the strength to support you yet. You will need a walking stick or something similar until you can build the strength up."

Aõ nodded in agreement. "I will try every day for as long as I can to strengthen my body. I have to forage for food for her."

Ani and Little Big Boy in simultaneous curiosity replied, "Her?"

Aõ nodded her head emphatically. "I have decided this chick is female and her name will be Atua."

As the next few days drifted past, Aõ, true to her word, was out the front or back of the healing hut practising her walk. It was a slow and painful process as she retrained her body to move.

Little Big Boy, meanwhile, tasked with grub finding, had developed an ingenious technique for discovering huge bugs and the tastiest of new shoots for Atua.

"Where do you find such nutritious foods?" enquired Aõ as she pounded the grubs and shoots into a slurry to feed Atua, who was trilling loudly. The chick had been standing and peering into the corner of the hut, pecking at small insects just on the inside of the wall. At the sound of Aõ's voice, Atua began making its haphazard way across the room. Little Big Boy, seated on Aõ's bed, pulled his legs up off the floor, trying not to make it obvious that he was afraid of the gigantic chick.

"I am clever, Aõ," he replied, brushing his hands down his body in pride. "I am using the foraging powers of the pigs to unearth the grubs which I steal from them, as well as their astute noses to locate the newest shoots of plants. It really is a breeze," he proudly stated as he watched, with eyes wide in fear, the bird stalk its way around the room.

He added with a shiver, "Aõ, that bird is already so big, she's quite terrifying."

Aδ looked at Atua. "She is so beautiful; it is her fluffy plume that makes her look so big. I am sure that will fall out soon and her real feathers will grow. Then she will be taller rather than round; that is what I have seen and this is also what Ahan has told me."

Little Big Boy sat up straighter at Ahan's name. "He has been to see you?" he inquired.

Aδ nodded as she held a heavy narrow cup filled with the fresh grub slurry in her hand for Atua to feed from.

"Yes he comes to see me as often as he can, which has been less and less these last couple of weeks; I assume it is because of the preparation to visit the Bush Tribe."

#

Ahan had indeed been preparing for the delegation; this was not an average party heading for a hunt or to meet another tribe on a casual basis. The integrity of the Emerald Water Tribe had been questioned and Amaro had heard the veiled threat behind the unhappy words the scouts recounted on return from the Bush Tribe.

Amaro's people would not be safe moving around the forest ranges or near the waterways until this matter had been laid to rest. Amaro would not have his reputation slighted and the safety of his people jeopardised. Therefore, an official delegation with well-prepared dialogue and a show of strength to remind the Bush Tribe who they were dealing with and making accusations against would be organised.

A few days earlier, Ahan examined the bodies of the young men found gutted in the outskirts of the lower hunting fields.

"They were not so young that they would have not been able to defend themselves," surmised Ahan. The sinew ropes had dried to a stiffness around the arms of the men so Ahan began soaking the intestines to soften them up. He respectfully piled them back into their respective body cavities. As Ahan worked, he saw the double-tied knots of flax cabling that secured the men's wrists that had been hidden underneath the overlaying intestines.

"So, they had been subdued, tied with flax cabling, gutted whilst still alive, and their intestines wound around their arms. For all this to happen, there must have been more than one man, even more than two men, to ensure they couldn't escape their excruciating fate," surmised Ahan, worried more than ever for where this train of thought was taking him. It was a short thought process that led him to Aõ, Little Big Boy, and the great risks that were hovering around them.

With a deep sigh and slight shake of his intricately designed head, Ahan knew he needed to set a contingency plan up to manage Aõ and Little Big Boy's safety whilst he was away.

The delegation that Ahan was part of would return the bodies of the young men to the Bush Tribe, who were being treated as respectfully as any member of the Emerald Water Tribe would be. After Ahan's examination, he packed the bodies with sweetened herbs that absorbed and reduced the smell of decay emanating from the corpses. As he began the suturing, he pulled the stiffened, blanched sides of the stomach back together, Ahan noted a sharp stone needle jutting out from under the right rib, the tip puncturing into the degraded lung tissue. Ahan, with the tip of his index finger and thumb, carefully eased the stone needle from its muscular bed and held it up in the dim light. This was not the first time he had seen something similar to this; the only difference between the needle he found buried in Leani in almost the same spot and this needle, was this one was shorter. Ahan looked closer at the flattened end. It appeared to have snapped off, leaving a five-centimetre tip embedded in the body of the young man.

That evening, Ahan paid a visit to Aõ and Atua.

As Ahan entered, he pushed aside the beaded curtain to step into the bedroom area occupied by Aõ, Ahan noted how large the chick had grown in a few short weeks, nodding his head in satisfaction at the bird, who was already showing signs of protectiveness over Aõ and territorial aggression towards him as he walked into Aõ's bed space. Atua squawked aggressively at Ahan and began fluttering its stunted wings to have its stubby unformed feathers rise up in an attempt to appear bigger.

"That is a pretty display, Atua," said Ahan as he walked past, petting the bird on the head as it pecked menacingly at him. Ahan pulled the stool out to sit opposite the bed Aõ was lounging on. The bird stomped its talons on the ground in an aggressive manner and continued to peck at Ahan's face, which was now at the same height as the standing bird. Aõ watched on in amusement as Ahan, yet to greet her, focused all his attention on the bird. Ahan reached down into his satchel pulling a pouch out.

There, in his hand, was the carefully woven grass that Ahan cut from where Aõ had been found almost dead. The grass was now dried and stained brown from the blood that soaked it so many moons ago. Ahan put it in front of the bird's face and the bird quickly began devouring the tasty grass. Ahan muttered some esoteric words, pressing the place between Atua's eyes and beak with his index finger. The bird closed its eyes as the pressure point was triggered and a low thrumming of enjoyment began vibrating deep in its throat. When Ahan released the pressure, he scratched Atua's neck and the bird arched its head in pleasure.

Ahan then turned his attention to Aõ, looking intently at her stroking his hair back into the Mohawk style he wore for casual encounters.

"There is so much that I haven't told you, believing that it was better that you did not know. It was a mistake on my behalf to try and protect you by keeping you in the dark. I see now that this has only led you to feel confused and fearful of your life without understanding why."

Ahan pulled from his satchel the throwing implement that Aõ made so many moons ago. "The creation of a weapon, be it for hunting or for protecting yourself, is a good indicator to me that, out of love, we made a mistake keeping the truth from you."

Aõ, eyes wide, stared at Ahan, curious at where this story was going. Ahan breathed in deeply, taking Aõ's hands in his warm ones, as he firmly pressed the throwing tool into her hands.

"You must continue practising with this."

"It will also help strengthen your arms and improve your aim," he stated as he sat back, leaving the throwing tool in Aõ's hands, fully knowing that it was against the Emerald Water Tribe's etiquettes that women should not be allowed to hunt or fight.

"I now find myself so short of time. I have left instructions with Warea to tell you about your heritage; it is time you knew about your mother.

"I have also asked Warea to stay with you here; I do not want you or Little Big Boy to be alone ever whilst I am away. Kai and some of the other guards will keep an eye out for you. As long as you remain inside the compound, you will be protected."

Aõ nodded her head, worried at his instructions. "But, Ahan, there is not enough food for Atua in the compound. Her food sources lay outside, in the lower grounds."

Ahan looked seriously at Aõ. "Aõ, you and Little Big Boy are not to go outside of the compound, you must find someone to get food for Atua for you."

Aõ looked dubiously at Ahan, brushing strands of hair from her face before taking a deep sigh. "My visitors are already scared of Atua and she's still a baby. Even Little

Big Boy, who is an excellent forager, is scared of her and he cannot go get her food, either."

Ahan smiled gently at Aδ. "Explain to Kai and the guards what Atua needs and they will help you.

"Warea will be here after the first meal, and the delegation leaves then also, so I will say my farewells to you now." He leaned in to hug her. Aδ pressed herself into his arms, breathing in his cinnamon scent, feeling the warmth, safety, and comfort of his strong arms.

"Thank you, Ahan, I will do as you say," she murmured into his chest.

Ahan smiled down at her. "I will see you when I return, remember my instructions," he reiterated as he extracted her from his arms.

## Chapter 14

## Strength of Arm, Not Strength of Mind

The morning that the delegation was to leave, Aõ found herself lacking food for Atua. The feeding situation was becoming desperate, as the guards who were to help keep Aõ safe, were not able to recognise the food sources for the growing bird. As Atua became hungrier, the bird became more destructive in the small room, drilling holes in the walls with her pecking beak and raking shallow holes in the ground of the bedroom with her talons.

"They are so stupid," stated Little Big Boy, after watching one of the guards deliver a half-hearted finding of brittle branches for Atua.

"It is not their fault, Little Big Boy," sighed Aõ, "They are guards, not foragers, they do not understand what a growing chick needs for food, the guards are used to hunting the Moa down for us to eat, not feeding one like a pet." She shook her head at the poorly selected branches.

"We will have to go to the lower fields and source food for Atua ourselves," said Aõ.

"Ahhhh," began Little Big Boy, ready to begin a counterargument which was cut off by Aõ's raised hand.

"I know what Ahan instructed, but there is no choice, Atua will die if I do not feed her, and I will not let that happen," Aõ stated firmly.

"You can carry me to the lower field and I am able to walk now; Warea can come with us if she is free from her duties and so can one of the guards, we won't be long, it will just be a quick forage," she added, convinced that her plan was foolproof.

"And Rimachi and his crew, Aõ, what if they are out and about in the lower fields?" enquired Little Big Boy. "What will we do then?"

"We will be safe with Warea and a guard, he cannot do anything, also he is caught up with the functioning and running of the tribe, he will not be wandering around with his cronies like he used to when Amaro was here," nodded Aõ confidently.

Later that morning, Aõ, Little Big Boy, and Atua, with a leash fashioned from Little Big Boy's belt draped around her neck, made their way to find Warea.

At the back of the kitchen, they found Warea deep to her elbows in sweet potato. Without even approaching her, Aõ and Little Big Boy could see she would not be free to go to the lower fields. They turned around and began their way slowly to find a guard escort.

"Hello, Patua," said Aõ, to a stocky, tattooed guard who looked down his nose with a deep frown at the two individuals standing before him.

The man called Patua raised his eyebrows in surprise and his frown travelled to the corners of his mouth when he saw Atua wandering around at the end of the leash.

"We need an escort, Patua, to the lower fields. We won't be gone long, we just need to forage for some food for my bird," began Aõ.

Patua shook his head once. "I am not assigned to do that, Aõ, you will need to find another escort." Patua turned his attention back to scanning the entrance and walkway to the inner compound.

Aõ and Little Big Boy approached three more guards around the compound to be told the same story.

Aõ turned to Little Big Boy in disappointment. "We don't have any other options; Atua needs to eat today."

Little Big Boy began shaking his head. "I know, Aõ, but I am afraid."

The two friends began the sloping walk down the path to the lower fields; Little Big Boy carrying Aõ on his back for short periods while she caught her breath. Aõ leaned over one of his shoulders, smiling in humour as she felt her feet bounce off the ground as Little Big Boy stomped his way along.

As they arrived at the edge of the lower fields, Aõ was pleasantly surprised to see so many people out foraging about, sharing food and new mothers letting their children play in the warm sunshine. Her heart ached at the peaceful scene; how she had missed these simple things that made up life, getting her hands dirty, the feel of grass between her toes, the cool fresh breeze just touched with a hint of warmth blowing through her hair. The women had watched the trio's slow progress down the path with Atua on a leash but uncontrollably darting crazily from one side of the path to the other, squawking in her loud, raucous screech at the delicious insects sunning themselves on the stems of grass and shrubs that lined the well-worn path to the upper compound. Aõ tugged the leash to pull Atua back into line when they reached the bottom, noticing the mothers herding their children away in safety from the unusual trio.

"You can put me down now, Little Big Boy," said Aõ, tapping him on his back.

"With pleasure," he grunted, dropping his arms to his sides which had been gripping Aõ's legs to let her slide down his back to the short distance to the ground.

"You are heavier than you look, Aõ, and that bird is a monster—impossible to control," he complained, leaning back with his hands on his hips to stretch out his spine.

Aõ looked sideways at him, unsure if he was being serious or not. She punched him lightly in the arm and they both laughed at his dry sense of humour. "Come, we must go in that direction." Aõ pointed off to the furthest corner of the field.

"Of course, we do," Little Big Boy sighed in resignation, rolling his eyes, as he slung his arm across her shoulders to help Aõ walk.

#

The walk took most of the morning to locate the field that was the primary grazing ground of the Moa. Both Aõ and Little Big Boy stepped quietly, trying to not make any unnecessary noises when they spotted the gigantic avians in the distance.

Atua, already excited by the excursion outside, began a rapid run back and forth, running to the length of the leash, almost pulling Aõ off her feet.

Atua's attention was fixed on the birds in the distance and her squawking became a long, drawn-out call that Aõ had never heard before.

"Aõ, she knows her own kind, she is not happy being leashed, you should let her go before those Moa come over to investigate. They may not be happy having one of their own contained by a human," suggested Little Big Boy, nervously pointing in the direction of the flock, watching Atua's unhappy behaviour escalate.

Atua began scratching at the ground with her talons, concentrating her power to lurch forward in bursts, attempting to break free from the leash from Aõ's firm grip.

"She may not come back, Little Big Boy," exclaimed Aõ, trying to control the oversized bird at the end of the makeshift leash.

"What happens if the other birds attack her?" added Aõ as she pulled back on the leash with both hands attempting to control Atua.

"I do not think you have a choice now," said Little Big Boy, his eyes widening, his hand jerking in a pointing motion to emphasise the flock of Moa who were now making their way across the field to investigate all the noise.

Aõ looked up, sucking her breath in awe, noting how much bigger the cautiously approaching birds were to Atua.

Aõ knew that the birds would not tolerate the presence of a human and most likely move into attack mode.

Aõ sighed, deeply regretting her decision to bring Atua to the grazing grounds.

She began loosening the leash to slide it up and over the bird's head.

Little Big Boy had started a nervous jig, bouncing from one foot to the other as the giant birds got closer.

"Hurry up, hurry up! I want to live today," he urged, looking frantically around for a place to hide.

"Under the log, Little Big Boy, scrape the leaves out," replied Aõ with tears in her eyes as she watched Atua begin running towards the flock.

They clambered quickly underneath the huge rotting log to watch the outcome of the birds' interactions.

Atua ran around in circles, appearing to be unsure of what to do, darting close then running away in fear. The birds circled Atua to inspect her from all sides. There was nowhere for the small juvenile to go.

One large brown Moa, in particular, leaned in, tilting its head from side to side, calling to Atua with a soft guttural trill.

From behind the inquisitive bird, came another infant just as fluffy and around the same size as Atua. The two birds stood eye to eye, shrieking at each other.

Aõ could see this miniature Atua lookalike bird had the start of new quills beginning to form upon the wings. The beak was black rather than pink like Atua's, and its head had the start of iridescent skin beginning to glow where the baby plume had fallen out.

Little Big Boy began elbowing Aõ sharply in the ribs at the sedate interactions occurring between the birds.

"See there, Aõ, they do not kill their own; Atua seems to be quite safe," he whispered nodding towards the exchange in front of them.

Aõ, not exactly happy that her baby had so easily integrated into the local avian flock, felt her heart melt with a profound sense of loss as she watched her beloved pet begin following the behaviours of her newly adopted family. Aõ pursed her lips together to blow the trill whistle that she had used in the hut to call Atua to her. Atua did not look up or indicate that she heard Aõ's call.

Aõ swallowed the painful lump that had developed in her throat and let the tears pour down her face, as she realised that there was nothing she could do to retrieve her baby, as the flock began grazing and moving its way back across the field.

"Come, Aõ, we should go, Atua will be fine here, and we can come back tomorrow," suggested Little Big Boy, sliding his arm around her in a comforting embrace, pulling her to him.

Aõ, leaning into him, thankful for the small comfort, nodded her head, wiping the tears roughly off her cheeks as Little Big Boy climbed out from under the log. Aõ reached out to take Little Big Boy's hand for assistance, to scramble up and out from beneath the log.

They stood for a few minutes, brushing the damp leaf litter from their clothing.

Aõ looked up in sadness one last time at the flock in the distance. It was almost as if Atua hadn't spent all those weeks with her, as if the bond that they developed was false.

The sad pair began their slow way back into the undergrowth. As they pushed the branches of a small, stunted tree away from their path, they slipped carefully past, to find themselves surrounded by a group of young men spread out along the path in front of them. Standing directly in the middle of the trail, with a sneer on his face, was Fat Knuckles.

#

From before Amaro's and Ahan's delegation of peace had left to return the bodies of the two dead boys, Rimachi had been planning his own rules around how his warriors, with him as the chief, would remould the etiquette of the Emerald Water Tribe people.

He was sick of the formal discussions happening every week that allowed the various cultural groups of men, women, and children who had joined them during the wayfarers' journey.

The opportunity to offer up the traditions that they had grown up with and valued from their old countries; to become adopted into their new emerging Emerald Water Tribe's practices and tribal lore.

No more discussion over whom it related to, men, women, children, elders. How would this practice benefit the tribe? What were the spiritual meanings behind the practice or song? What was it designed to teach or enforce?

It was taking years to embed common practice into the Emerald Water Tribe and Rimachi had had enough.

The Emerald Water Tribe just needed to be told what to do and if someone did something out of line, they should be punished. End of story.

Every evening in their men's hut, Rimachi had been quietly preaching his views and vision of the new Emerald Water Tribe amongst his men. He had groomed his men into voicing his philosophy to their families and embedded their loyalty through initiation.

Finding a man's weakness through conversation and observation and then exploiting it, was a talent Rimachi developed quickly in his early years.

As he grew older, Rimachi discovered a distasteful commonality amongst all the men, regardless of their age group—the beating and violent acts perpetrated against a woman.

The idea of causing violence towards a woman, the precious ones that nurtured this generation and created the next generation, was one of the most uncomfortable topics Rimachi had uncovered to date.

The persuasion to commit acts of violence against women to prove loyalty had taken many nights to convince the men to attempt it.

Rimachi enjoyed every minute twisting and coercing the men to his way of thinking. He could see in their eyes, their staunch stance against the concept of violence breaking down over the weeks.

The death of Leani had been the tipping point when the men saw that no repercussions were forthcoming.

A spur-of-the-moment decision by Rimachi and a few suggestions of harm delivered under the guise of fun was all it took to get the perpetrators moving.

Liosi—the man that had tripped Leani, had been wracked with guilt and grief following her death—a satisfying outcome, thought Rimachi, aware that Leani was pregnant and how close his men's group and break in the philosophy of cultural inclusion had come to discovery. It hadn't taken much for Rimachi to shut Liosi's distress down, with threats to reveal Liosi's role in Leani's death and his own death if he spoke to anyone about their involvement.

From that point, the men fell uneasily into beating women to show their strength and loyalty towards Rimachi.

The killing of the two Bush Tribe boys by the men's group created an unexpected advantage and opportunity for Rimachi to push his agenda further.

Rimachi's group were out hunting for small game when they had stumbled across the two boys from the Bush Tribe by chance.

The boys had approached Rimachi's group with hands extended in friendship, looking to trade on food and knowledge about the shared hunting grounds. All had gone well with the friendship exchange; a fire was lit, all the men pulled up logs to sit and talk, whilst their successful kills of miniature pigs roasted on the spits over the fire.

It was going well with the exchange, laughter and comfortable friendships were developing, until Rimachi walked up behind one of the unsuspecting Bush Tribe men, drawing a sharp combat club, and sliced it across his throat, creating an opening from ear to ear.

A blitz attack that no one, except Rimachi, knew was going to happen. A blitz attack that changed the dynamics of the men's group forever.

#

Even now, Rimachi revelled in the power he felt at the taking of a life. Powerful, but not as powerful as taking the life of the second Bush Tribesman, who, with utter confusion and then fear in his face, watched the gurgling demise of his friend sitting next to him. The second Bush Tribesman jumped up in an attempt to escape from the group but was quickly subdued by Rimachi's men.

Next time, Rimachi thought to himself, I want to see a line of people with the same degree of fear on their faces.

I want to plunge my fist into a chest, feel the beating heart and squeeze it into submitting to me while I watch the life fade from their eyes.

The thought of controlling the moment of life and death made his manhood jerk with arousal. Rimachi flashbacked to his assault on Aõ.

Her utter rejection of him and his being was exacerbated by Aõ spitting into his face. The subsequent assault he inflicted on her body has caused a catastrophic effect in his thought processes. He had always been given what he wanted when he wanted it.

The spitting in his face had triggered a sensation of excitement. His groin pulled in semi-hardness and his breath quickened as he thought about the power he had over another living being. The sounds and feel of his fists striking another body with power was the same sensation as plunging himself into an untouched woman. He could no longer do one without the other.

To have someone deny him was a new experience. An exciting experience. An experience he wanted again and again. Rimachi wanted to build on what he had felt. Bland assaults on women no longer held the excitement they used to for him.

Rimachi needed more, as his evolution into a sadistic killer began to gather momentum.

#

Rimachi had been in training grounds with his men, practising spear work and close combat with short-hand clubs.

The ground had been churned with plumes of dust rising up with their vigorous thrusting, turning and pounding. Rimachi and his men were covered in thin sheets of perspiration and dirt when Amaro, the Chief of the Emerald Water Tribe—his father, came to stand off to one side, watching the young men work through their routines.

Amaro noted how Rimachi would correct, offer advice, and demonstrate to the men, improved techniques to speed up their attack moves. Rimachi practised just as hard as the men. It was easy for Amaro to see the respect and loyalty in the way the men listened and returned comment to Rimachi's instructions.

Amaro could feel the swelling of pride growing in his chest as he watched his beloved son demonstrate his leadership skills without realising his father was there.

#

Amaro had been quietly concerned at the suggestions of Rimachi's character following Ahan's visit to discuss the violent attacks on the Emerald Water Tribe women.

He began watching his son's behaviour around the compound over the last few weeks but had not noted anything out of the ordinary.

He inhaled a deep breath and allowed it to slowly escape his body, a sigh of relief that Ahan's concerns—who was not often wrong—appeared to be wrong this time. Amaro had swallowed down his worry and anxiety over Ahan's accusations, finally satisfied that Ahan, this time, was wrong.

Concluding that Ahan was wrong did not sit well with Amaro. He was curt and abrasive in his interactions with those around him, as his thoughts about Ahan played out. Throwing sticks from afar at the fire pit, making the flames leap up; his annoyance, he realised was directly because of Ahan. He relied on Ahan more than he would ever let on. Ahan had saved the Emerald Water Tribe on many occasions, not only during the journey to their new lands, when Mateo, the old chief, had died en route, when sickness and storms had almost killed them all, but also when they had first landed on their new land. Ahan had always managed to devise a plan that saved them all. Find the freshwater sources, discover edible plants and ways to capture the smaller quick-witted animals to supplement their diets.

The diet and health of the Emerald Water Tribe had also been better than that of the other tribes whilst travelling in their wayfarer crafts to their new land.

Maarkus, Ahan's father, had devised strategies to travel to each of the giant crafts to help with the health of the travellers, but it took precious time to manoeuvre safely between tribal crafts. With the unpredictable weather and ocean swells, sometimes it was not possible to get to the craft in need in time. Often it would take days to traverse the distance from one craft to the next—always with the fear that the smaller craft used by Maarkus may be swamped or smashed by the churning ocean between the larger crafts.

Within time, Ahan was also pulled from duties to be sent out amongst the wayfaring crafts to offer medicinal assistance. It was this practice that set up the concept of caregiver acolytes in their new world.

#

As Amaro watched Rimachi, he came to the spontaneous decision to allow his son to take the reins for the few short weeks that he would be away. It was a big move and a significant change from the normal practices of leaving the Tribe's welfare in the hands of the women elders.

Amaro had originally come to the training grounds to let Rimachi know he was leaving and the governance of the tribe as per usual, under the elders. He had wanted to speak directly with Rimachi, aware that Rimachi would be disappointed with this decision, having to wait again for an opportunity to prove himself.

Why not now? thought Amaro, as he watched Rimachi and his men laughing, smacking their hands and shoulders in friendly comradery as they worked through their training.

#

In the chill of the early morning, Rimachi pulled his cloak in closer around him and listened to the eerie farewell songs chanted by the elder women wishing safety for the departing delegation.

He breathed deep into his newfound sense of superiority.

His father had been easy to manipulate. His father saw from afar what he wanted to see—Rimachi, with his men, had been staging activities for the last few weeks, performing training drills with his men showing an intentional respect one would exhibit towards a fully initiated warlord; leadership skills Rimachi knew would inspire his father.

The day Amaro had told him he was leaving the tribal governance in his hands, Rimachi had known that Amaro was coming to the training grounds.

As Rimachi listened to the chanting songs of the elders, he crossed his arms and lifted his head higher in the cool morning air as he thought to himself of the first tasks he needed to commit himself to—ridding the tribe of evil influences.

At the top of that list were Aõ, Little Big Boy, and, if necessary, Warea—all the people that were important to Ahan.

#

As the delegation of peace disappeared from view, Rimachi and his men made their way over to the healing hut, intent on finalising the deaths of Aõ and Little Big Boy. As the men pushed past the complaining caregivers, they discovered that the primary targets, which had been sitting under his nose but inaccessible for so long, were nowhere to be found.

"Where are they?" demanded Aleki, grabbing the caregiver Mara by the throat and lifting her off the ground, pulling her face close to his.

Her eyes flashed in hatred at him whilst her hands grasped in desperation at his fingers harshly choking the breath from her. Aleki laughed once in spite, before opening his fingers, letting Mara drop heavily to the floor. Ani, who had been cowering in the corner eyeballing her son, and the throng of men with hostility, rushed over to Mara's side, helping her get to her feet.

"We do not know where Aõ and Little Big Boy are. They left at the same time the delegation did. We do not know where they have gone," yelled Ani in their direction.

"Now get out of here!" she screamed pointing towards the door.

The men looked to Rimachi who had stood in the doorway in silence as he watched the scene unfold. He raised his eyebrows at the men who began filtering out of the healing hut. Aleki, one of the last to leave, made a crouched lunge towards the women, making them flinch back in terror.

With a menacing growl at them, he hissed aggressively,

"Watch yourselves, caregivers, you are not protected as you once were. There are new rules now, be sure to stay within them or you will find yourself with more than a tender neck to recover from." He straightened himself to full height and headed towards the door with a sneer on his face.

Mara, now able to breathe, rubbed her neck, spitting in his direction. "I will poison all of you if another man comes near this hut. You will shit out your innards and I will watch, laugh, and dance in them before I feed them to the Moa," she hoarsely whispered back in retaliation.

"That's enough, Mara," scolded Ani gently who had been nodding in agreement. "Now clean up that spit off the floor."

Mara nodded her head. "I will, Ani, but we must do something to aid Aõ and Little Big Boy. Ahan has only just left and Rimachi is openly hunting them down; they are in danger just as Ahan predicted. We must mobilize all the caregivers and find them before Rimachi and his men do."

Ani breathed in deeply, contemplating Mara's request.

She nodded once. "Go find the acolytes, make sure they bring their satchels. I think we will need them for Aõ and Little Big Boy."

#

Rimachi ordered his men to begin a thorough search of the inner compound. His scouts returned to him, stating Warea was amongst the other women engaged in meal preparation and would most likely not be accessible until later in the evening.

This news irritated Rimachi even more.

Rimachi clicked his tongue and waved his hand in annoyance. "Well, find the two. There must be some trace as to where they went!"

It wasn't long before the gossip of the strange trio of Aõ, Atua, the Moa baby, and Little Big Boy in the lower hunting grounds had traversed to the upper compound.

Immediately upon hearing of them, Rimachi and his men, grabbing their weapons in military precision, began their run out of the upper compound and down the path to the lower levels.

It had taken some time and tracking to locate the path Aõ, Little Big Boy, and Atua had left.

Rimachi's excitement peaked when his targets suddenly appeared.

Almost immediately, Aõ and Little Big Boy disappeared back around the tree and out of sight.

Rimachi, with a forward hand signal to his men, ordered them to surround and capture the two friends.

He strode his way forward, taking his time, grinning in humour at how the next few hours would play out.

He wanted to enjoy every minute of watching the pain flow into their eyes, hearing their cries of agony as he burrowed his hand through their chest and up to their hearts.

Rimachi wondered if he could do both Aõ and Little Big Boy at the same time, could he watch each of them witnessing each other's suffering?

Yes, he decided, this was something he wanted to see.

#

# Chapter 15

# The Hunted and Protected

It didn't take long for Rimachi's men to chase down Aõ and Little Big Boy.

They made it to the edge of the Moa grazing field before the men tackled them both to the ground.

One of the men hauled Little Big Boy to his feet, punching him hard in the face, whilst another pulled Aõ to her feet by her hair.

Aõ squealed loudly in pain at the rough handling, grabbing with both hands at the larger male hand gripping her hair. She was punched hard in the stomach in an attempt to shut her up.

"It is nice to see you up and about, Aõ," said Rimachi as he walked sedately around the group. "I have been waiting a long time to see you, a very long time to spend some more time in your company," Rimachi added with a smile. In his hands, he held a small, sharp knife which he was using to clear out the filth under his fingernails.

"And your little half-man, half- pig friend here," he said pointing with the tip of his knife in the direction of Little Big Boy, "Always at your side; what a loyal annoying animal he is," he added sarcastically before plunging the knife into Little Big Boy's side.

Little Big Boy let out the loudest squeal of agony as his legs gave way, only to be held up by one of Rimachi's Henchmen. "Do not do this," begged Little Big Boy between his gasps of pain, as he clutched his side in an attempt to staunch the flow of blood.

"There is no quarrel between anyone here, we are all related through family ties, do not cause damage to us!" he begged the group. The men began to point and laugh as piss ran down Little Big Boy's leg.

Aõ, gasping for breath, had been slumped over, her hair tightly wound in Aleki's grip. With a sinking heart, Aõ knew their lives were over.

Aõ knew she was not strong enough physically or emotionally to survive another assault from Fat Knuckles. This time, she knew she would die—there would be no falling into unconsciousness this time, Fat Knuckles would ensure she would be painfully alert to all he did to her.

She raised her head in distress, trying to find a less painful position, when, in the corner of her blurry vision, saw a rapid motion moving across the field. As she blinked, screwing her eyes and face up to improve her sight, a loud squawking began resonating across the field.

Aõ inhaled quickly, her eyes darting from side to side, trying to make sense of the scene unfolding before her.

Unbeknown to Rimachi's men in their rush to secure Aõ and Little Big Boy, they had unwittingly captured them on the edge of the Moa's grazing fields.

They were unfamiliar with the lay of the land and the behaviours of the giant birds who were grazing calmly off to one side of the field.

Excited that they had finally tracked their quarry, the men had failed to scout the terrain as they would normally do.

Most of the men had their backs to the rapidly approaching Moa, unaware of the lethal danger they were now in.

Atua heard the cries of pain coming from Aõ and immediately turned away from her grazing new Moa family, to earnestly locate where Aõ was. With a raucous protective call, the diminutive Atua began a staunch trot in the direction of the human group, bringing the attention and presence of the entire Moa flock with her.

Aõ watched the Moa flock rushing towards the group of unsuspecting men. She began to giggle through her pain.

"You all need to leave now or you will die," she said to the group of men through her laughter.

"I am protected by Ahan and those he entrusted to keep me safe. This is the only chance you have to escape with your lives. If you do not let me and Little Big Boy go now, you will all die," Aõ stated with as much power as she could muster from the awkward posture she was in.

Fat Knuckles stepped forward with one fist raised and the other grasping Aõ by the front of her shirt and readied himself to punch her face into oblivion.

It was the last movement he made, before a gigantic bird leapt into the middle of the fray with both talons splayed before its body, outstretched to grab at Rimachi.

Hearing the guttural squawking, the men, including Rimachi, turned at this new unexpected attack. Rimachi had turned his upper torso towards the sounds, when a fully grown male Moa, with the deepest of black plume and razor-sharp talons, landed fully on him, embedding both claws deeply in his chest. he fell hard to the ground under the weight of the bird.

The bird began flapping its undersized wings to counterbalance its landing, pulled its claws up, and ripped chucks of flesh out of Rimachi's body.

, Unable to protect himself, began an unrelenting shrieking of agony at the unexpected suffering his body was enduring.

The men, completely surprised by the unexpected attack, fell into chaos as each scrambled to save themselves.

Atua, dodging the scrambling, fearful men, located her mother in the attack, and stood protectively over Aõ, squawking, hissing, and pecking repeatedly at anyone that came near, as Aõ lay on the ground trying to regain her breath.

The few men that had enough hunting presence attempted to move into a tight circle against the seven-foot birds. Those that didn't, choosing to run for safety, were pounced on and, whilst their screams of pain and agony still echoed across the field, were shredded and pecked beyond recognition.

None of Rimachi's men had stalked the Moa, if they had, they would have been able to anticipate the hunting behaviour of the bird and been able to protect themselves to some degree.

The birds systematically began running around the small group of humans, making false lunges at the men only to pull back at the last moment when a man stepped forward to counter the attack.

Once the Moa had drawn the unsuspecting men out into a larger circle with undefendable gaps, two of the largest birds moved towards the group of humans, drawing the attention of all the men with the diversional raucous shrieks and a show of razor-sharp talons, flapping wings, and snapping beaks. The group of men began shuffling forward in a line to face the danger coming at them leaving their backs exposed.

They did not see the attack coming from the birds which had quietly slipped in behind the group, moving off to the sides in the pretence of grazing.

One of the warriors felt a sudden thump to his back and looked down in surprise to see blood running in rivets from his shoulders and onto his chest. As he looked up incredulously, his face came eyeball to eyeball with that of a hissing Moa, its beak extended towards his face. The bird thrust its beak directly into his eye, plucking the ball roughly from the socket. As he began to shriek in horror and pain, the bird raked its razored claws down the man's chest, ripping open his stomach. Knowing the man was doomed, the Moa moved on to its next victim.

Aõ, hearing the cries of dying men all around her, rolled herself onto her side, looking frantically along the ground to where she had last seen Little Big Boy. There, on the grass, was a trail of blood disappearing into the undergrowth.

Aõ sat herself up, her head was spinning, making it hard to focus, as the ground lurched up and down around her. Her mouth fill with water as nausea and bile flooded in. She swallowed it down, awkwardly getting her knees under her body. She began crawling in the same direction as the blood trail, with Atua following behind.

As she made her slow way towards the undergrowth, she heard a hiss coming out from under the rotting log her and Little Big Boy had recently hidden under earlier that day. "Over here," came a hoarse whisper. Aõ lurched towards the log, rolling unceremoniously under it. Little Big Boy grabbed at her, pulling her deep beneath its trunk.

"I thought you were dead," he sobbed into her and the two friends hugged each other tightly.

"I thought you were too; you went quiet so quickly, I thought they had ended your life," Aõ replied, sobbing hard into his shoulder at the thought of how close she had come to losing her best friend.

"I don't know how we survived all that, but it is good to know that Ahan chose the best protector for you," said Little Big Boy.

Aõ nodded in agreement, "I thought I had lost Atua but I didn't. We are lucky."

Little Big Boy, covered in damp broken stinking leaves, looked with contempt at Aõ and responded, "You call this lucky?"

"I have a hole in my side which will leave a terrible scar on my beautiful body—my skin is ruined," lamented Little Big Boy. "And you have hair missing from your head," he added rubbing his hand over Aõ's head.

"We could have died a terrible death, Little Big Boy, she replied. "Fat Knuckles would have slaughtered me while you watched, knowing that the same thing would happen to you." Aõ stared at him, eyes wide in seriousness.

"Oh, yes, there's that too" replied Little Big Boy flipping the hand not holding his wounded side in a nonchalant manner. Aõ shot him a grin at his facetiousness.

The two friends waited quietly in their safe haven under the log until all the sounds of the Moa had disappeared from hearing.

"Time to go," whispered Aõ, scrambling past the damp leaf litter to slowly haul herself up and out from under the log. Stooping over with hands on her legs to catch her breath for a minute, she began her slow limp back towards the carnage on the field.

"What are you doing?" whispered Little Big Boy hoarsely.

"You are going in the wrong direction, home is this way!" he stated, emphasising the direction by waving his hands in earnest, indicating towards the path into the undergrowth behind them.

"These are men of the Emerald Water Tribe," replied Aõ. "We cannot leave them, some may still be alive, and we have to help get them away from here."

"We will end up dead like them, Aõ," retorted Little Big Boy, who followed grudgingly, running up to slide his arm under Ao's to help her walk.

"And how much help will you be? You can barely walk yourself," he grumbled.

Aõ nodded in agreement, pushing him away. "You are right, Little Big Boy, you will need to go back to the compound for help. I will stay here and at least try to relieve some of their suffering, if I find anyone alive," she added, dubious in her own optimism.

"I agree," he replied, quickly unhooking his support arm from hers. "Please be careful; I do not want to find you ripped apart out there either," he said with a quick hug before making his way hastily towards the thick bank of shrubs that hid their pathway home.

Aõ walked from body to body, looking for any indication of life. Aõ choked back her anguish and shook her head in sadness as the tears rolled silently down her face; she realised how successful the Moa had been at eliminating humans.

When she eventually got to Fat Knuckles, she was surprised to see blood bubbling up from his lips in bursts as he took painful breaths in an attempt to stay alive. Aõ fell to her knees in relief that someone had survived. She leaned in close to see what she could do to help him.

Aõ peered at his ruined body, seeing through the deep gashes, the red of internal organs and white of intestines as Rimachi, with his hands, desperately tried to hold everything together.

"Help is coming, Rimachi. It will be here soon, please hold on," said Aõ in despair as she looked around to see what she could use to help relieve his pain and ease his breathing. She bundled a ripped piece of clothing under his head, attempting to raise it up, making him breathe easier.

Rimachi groaned and began taking breaths in short gasping motions as he tried to get more air into his lungs.

"I will kill you, sister," he panted out in short bursts. "You will not succeed as chief of this tribe." He struggled to get his sentences out as blood continued to bubble from his mouth.

Aõ wiped his mouth clear of blood with the side of her sleeve.

"Do not talk, please, just try to save your energy, the caregivers will be here soon," she replied. Aõ was incredulous that his hatred for her was so ingrained, that, even this close to death, he would pour his hatred towards her in his last breaths.

"I do not understand what you are talking about, Rimachi," she added as an afterthought. "We are not siblings," she included with curiosity.

Rimachi eyeballed her with disgust. "You killed Amaro's second wife, one of our mothers, you stupid animal hole. Implanted in our mother by the gods? I know this is a lie," he spat blood at her.

"You were implanted in Amaro's second wife by Ahan," he hissed at her, using the small amount of strength to try and push her away. "My father incurred an injury to his groin which made it impossible for him to have more children, you were an experiment to grow the chieftain lineage. No one was supposed to know, hence the story of your miraculous birth. It was obvious from the moment you appeared that you were not my father's offspring. He chose to disown you on the death of our mother."

Aõ pulled herself back at his retort, confused by his statement. Her thoughts whirled in her head, making it hard for her to make meaning about what he said.

In an attempt to buy time to digest what Fat Knuckles told her, Aõ busied herself with scrounging a gourd of water dropped by one of Rimachi's men earlier in the chaos.

The confusion of her life and all the missing pieces began to fall into place at the raw truth of Rimachi's words. She carefully lifted his head to dribble the tepid water into his mouth.

He swallowed painfully before spurting more blood at her.

"You need to kill yourself and kill your father for the dishonesty and lies he perpetrated through the tribe to build his value. He raped my father's second wife and implanted you in her, and you killed her with your birth," sputtered Rimachi, choking on the rush of words and shortness of breath, as he voiced his thoughts in earnest before sinking back, exhausted, turning his face away from her tendering.

Aõ shook her head in disbelief but could feel the truth in her heart of his words. Is this why he hated me so much? she thought. I believed for so long that his hatred for me was just because of the way I looked. Aõ looked down at the dying man before her and experienced a flash of distaste towards him.

With drying tears on her face, the sympathy she had felt towards Rimachi and the men of the Emerald Water Tribe lying in this field of death, turned into sour contempt.

Aõ looked down at Fat Knuckles.

"From the earliest of age, Ahan was groomed by our forefather, Maarkus, and Mateo, your grandfather, to ensure the survival of the originals of the Emerald Water Tribe. He did save them many times and is exalted with accolades of love and fierce pride because he found this land first, because he saved us!" she pleaded at the dying Rimachi. "Why do you hate him so much?"

Rimachi reached up, gripping her by the front of her shirt with his bloody hand, pulling her close with the last of the strength in him.

"Because you are both wrong in your thinking, you will kill us all with your inclusion of so many people and their ways, diluting our tribal identity," he murmured at her before sinking down into unwanted unconsciousness.

Aõ sat back on her heels, looking down at the man who would be her chief if he survived this attack. Bile rose in her mouth as her own hatred began festering in the pit of her stomach, turning to acid, making her mouth water. Aõ turned her head, vomit exploding out of her and on the ground.

As she wiped her mouth with the back of her sleeve, she turned back to Fat Knuckles.

She was appalled at where his paradigm of hatred sat within the doctrine of the Emerald Water Tribe.

"I hope you die on this field," she whispered harshly at him. "If you live, I hope you will be maimed and crippled so you do not advance to chief. I hope you cannot assist with the wellbeing of the tribe because of your injuries. I wish you pain forever!" Aõ hissed at him, smacking the ground in frustration with the palms of her hands.

Aõ got herself up painfully from Fat Knuckles' side and began making her limping way back to the pathway that led to home, when the caregivers burst out from the trees, in speed and onto the killing field. They spread out in a coordinated sweep to begin quietly and discreetly searching the bodies.

# Chapter 16

# The Truth Behind it All

Aõ felt the beams of sunlight flash across her face as she began regaining consciousness. She pressed her eyelids together firmly, easing the tears out from between them in response to the bright light.

Aõ came fully awake in her bed, in the familiar comforting room of the healing hut. She turned her head at the small noises coming from across the room and saw in delight Atua pecking at the small bugs burrowing between the wall panels.

As she moved, Warea jumped into wakefulness. She had been dozing at the bedside for how long, she had no idea.

She reached her hand out to gently place it on top of Warea's. Warea looked at Aõ in relief and sadness. "I am sorry," she began. "I am sorry we didn't tell you sooner, about your heritage, beyond that of a gift from Ahan. We kept the truth from you to protect you, Aõ," she sobbed in sorrow and guilt.

"Ahan asked me to tell you the truth about who you are and, in my fear, I did not, I left you alone and vulnerable. You almost died a second time because of my fear," Warea sobbed as the words escaped her mouth in a haphazard way.

#

Aõ patted Warea's hand. "It is all right, I am not dead, and Rimachi is. It has worked out better than I could have thought. I do not have to worry about him threatening and hurting me anymore," said Aõ.

Warea clutched Aõ to her, kissing her forehead and averted her eyes from Aõ, moving the subject back to Ahan and Aõ's history.

Nodding her head she said, "I promised Ahan I would tell you when you awoke and, if you were strong enough, I would begin your story so you understand your heritage." She wiped the tears of remorse from her cheeks with the back of her hand and began to speak.

Aõ nodded her head. "Rimachi told me something about sharing the same mother and this was the reason for him hating me so much," she recounted.

Warea nodded her head in sadness, stroking Aõ's hair back from her forehead. "This is true but there is more."

"Your mother was my beloved daughter, my only child," began Warea as her eyes took on a teary far-away look as she began to recount her past. Her hand plucked absently at the blanket covering Aõ, pulling at loose threads as she gathered her thoughts.

"We were from an island very far from here." She began shaking her head as the memories flowed forth.

"If the watercrafts the Emerald Water Tribe's people were in had not been blown so badly off course, we would not be here.

"I was very young when your grandfather died—he drowned whilst trying to retrieve some delicacy food from the ocean floor. I was grieving for him and everywhere on the island was a reminder of him to me. I thought a number of times to walk out into the ocean and join his spirit or throw myself off the highest point into the ocean to be with him. I was on the cliff face, gathering my courage to take the final step forward, when the giant watercrafts appeared on the horizon. It was as if the ocean gods had come to save me from the pit of despair I was in.

"Your mother, Te-ata, was a young girl about the same age you are now. I made my way down the cliff to the beach with your mother next to me.

"We waited and watched as the smaller vessels from the giant watercraft made their way onto the beach. Mateo, Maarkus, Ahan's father, and both Amaro and Ahan were the first to touch the shore.

"I remember seeing them laughing and clapping each other on the shoulder as if they had achieved something amazing. They were looking about with open, wondering eyes like children," she said with a smile.

"They looked so different from us. Their skin was brown but a different colour of light brown. Where our hair was black and wavy, the wayfarers' was coarse, black, and straight.

"Their noses were flat and arrow-shaped, where ours are broad but pointed. They looked like us but were not. Their eyes were black rather than shades of brown and their clothing was nothing we had ever seen before."

"Leather, leaves, fabrics, and weaving styles we had never encountered before; they were exciting to meet from so many aspects.

"Some of their words we could understand but it took some time to begin speaking in complete sentences without the use of gestures and dance.

"But it only took a few days before the boundaries of friendship and peace had been established and the young people were allowed to mingle. Ahan and Amaro saw Te-ata and she saw Ahan. I could feel the magnetism between them both as they stood there pretending to listen to the promises of peace and friendship being offered by Mateo of the Emerald Water Tribe to our island chief. I could see their eyes searching each other's faces as if to commit them to memory.

"I remember looking discreetly at Te-ata as she stood next to me with her head turned in curiosity towards Ahan. I could almost feel them building a connection of energy as they stood there staring at each other, becoming aware of each other." Warea gripped her hands together leaning forward, eyes closed as if to immerse her face into the memory.

"As I saw the cautious grins begin on both their faces, I knew then that they were destined to be together and, despite my grief, I was thankful for a chance to focus on the future that included happiness and life."

Warea stroked Að's hair. "You look so like Te-ata, your face, body, and inner strength are the same as hers, though you share your father's hair colour, nose, and eye colour, you represent both of them in your looks and caring ways," she said gently.

Warea paused to take a deep breath and continued her story.

"Your mother and Ahan were to be together—so I thought. It was as if the gods and universal energies had made two parts to fit together perfectly—this was Ahan and Te-ata.

"So, it came as a great surprise that Amaro declared his intentions to Mateo, Maarkus, and our chief, to take Te-ata as his second wife. An opportunity to show bondage and build ties between our tribes. An opportunity that the chiefs could not throw away.

"Maarkus told Ahan a few nights before the marriage ceremony, as I did to Te-ata. They did not take well to the news," said Warea with a shake of her head and a half smile on her face. "I tried to tell Te-ata that there were ways of still having what she wanted without having to break the bonds of family and friendship—if she could be discreet. But she was young and did not understand or want to play the games of infidelity."

Aõ, surprised at the candidness of the conversation, shifted her position to resettle, nodding her head, encouraging Warea to continue.

Warea nodded back in response. "Your mother was tied in a bonding ceremony to Amaro, all the while staring intensely at Ahan with love all over her face, and he staring back with a broken heart, unable to find a solution for their predicament.

"To complicate matters, Amaro already had another wife—a first wife—Rimachi's mother, who was an original Emerald Water Tribe member. When they arrived on the shores of our island, Rimachi was two seasons born. She was not happy with the new arrangements of a second wife," Warea said with a slight smile as she glanced at Aõ.

Warea continued with her story. "Needless to say, the first wife was happy when she discovered that Te-ata had no interest in Amaro, even more so when the injury to Amaro happened."

Warea took a glass from the small table next to the bed and had a sip of the lukewarm water before placing the cup down to continue.

"One evening, on the giant watercraft, Amaro was showing Rimachi how to hold a spear when the water moved, making the craft lurch forward. Rimachi, new to walking, stumbled on the wake of the wave and buried the tip of the spear he had in his hands deep into Amaro's upper thigh, causing damage to his manhood.

"We left three moons after the wayfarers arrived—two moons after the other watercraft, waiting for the tides to move in our favour in hopes of catching up.

"The journey of the wayfarers is another story, Aõ, that I promise to recount to you on another day," finished Warea, patting the bed. Aõ nodded, eyes wide in interest at hearing another version of the travels.

"Your mother and Amaro's first wife became quite good friends, but it was distressing for them both that Amaro chose Te-ata night after night in an attempt to give him a child without success.

"In the end, Mateo and Amaro spoke with Maarkus and Maarkus did the one thing that he knew would make his son and Te-ata happy.

"On the dark of the moon and under the guise of ritual, he delivered medicines to strengthen Amaro's manhood, insisting he refrain from any contact with women for at least two moon cycles." Warea paused in her retelling and lowered her head to take a deep breath before continuing her story.

"He also isolated Ahan and Te-ata on a small craft, giving Ahan instructions on which medicines Te-ata was to take to strengthen her womb—to make it ready for receiving the gift of life.

"Those of us that had seen Te-ata and Ahan together knew what kind of medicines Te-ata was going to receive and, I am sure, so did Maarkus," said Warea with a grin, nudging the blankets tucked around Aõ in jest.

"And I was correct—by the end of that first moon and halfway into the second, Te-ata was with child."

#

"We were blessed with auspicious weather for the remainder of the trip to our new land, though we had no idea we were so close. It took us still another seven moon cycles to reach here, and your mother was so close to giving birth to you. She would tell me of how hard you used to kick her," laughed Warea as her reminiscing took on a light-hearted telling.

"As soon as Ahan's discovery of a new land began to circulate around the vessels, we all clambered along one side of the watercraft, tilting it dangerously to one side in the water.

"The first thing we saw was the circling of birds and the longest, whitest cloud stretching from the peak of a mountain along the entire length of the land. It was breathtaking. We were all convinced that this was the land the ancients had promised us so long ago.

"As we made land and the men deemed it safe, we disembarked near the mouth of a river, and that is when we saw the light bouncing off its surface, radiating a deep green colour.

"I remember how the ladies began singing in joy at this new discovery, which seemed to confirm that we had finally arrived.

"Your mother—desperate to stretch her legs and for a cool drink of fresh water—made her way with a small group of women and some guards in tow, moved further along the banks, splashing water at each other and laughing in happiness. Te-ata waded out further, looking to relieve the heaviness of her belly in the cool water. She sank deep- losing her footing and disappeared under the surface. One of the guards rescued her, pulling her up by her hair, spluttering and tearful at how close she had come to dying on the first day of being on the new lands. In her attempt to find something to help her get to the surface, she grasped a stone.

"As she lay on the river bank catching her breath, one of the other women pointed to the stone she had in her hand. It was a deep green, emerald stone, something we had never seen before."

#

"On return to the watercraft, Te-ata, in remorse for her near-death encounter that could have ruined the decision to stay, presented the emerald rock to the chiefs.

"It was this discovery—we now call the sacred stone—that made the tribal chiefs decide that, regardless of whether there were people already here or not, we would be staying and we would fight to stay if need be.

"There were too many signs that made it impossible for us to walk away from here.

"We spent the next few weeks foraging and exploring the area. We did not find any other people.

"The navigators of the watercraft now used their skills to find us an advantage point to build our compounds. They had just begun to map out the area when you decided it was time to arrive." Warea looked at Aõ in sadness.

"Your mother struggled for days to give birth to you. In the end, she did not have enough strength to push you from her body. Ahan had to cut you from her womb. You lived, healthy and squalling, but Te-ata died not long after.

"You have been in mine and Ahan's care ever since," finished Warea with a deep sigh of release, pleased that, finally, she told the story of her origins to Aõ.

Aõ lay back on her bed, watching Atua flitting back and forth, dipping her beak into the wall at the small bugs that resided in the crevices of the poles. Aõ waited patiently for Warea to continue, finally realising that Warea was not going to say any more.

Aõ felt the scowl begin on her face and quickly swallowed in an attempt to change the disgruntled look.

This was it? This was all she was going to be told.

Aõ looked down at her bed covers, thinking about the tale Warea just told her. All this pain, all this suffering she endured at the hands of Fat Knuckles, was because Ahan had taken her mother? Because they loved each other?

Aõ was surprised at how deeply disappointed she felt by the retelling of her birth. Warea's version told her nothing of substance. Why did Rimachi hate her so much?

Why was a falsehood told about her birth? Details glossed over by Warea's telling.

Aõ looked suspiciously at Warea. There was more to the wayfarer's tale and her being here than what Warea was saying. Aõ could feel the unspoken words lying like grey clouds between them.

What was Warea not saying? thought Aõ. Why was she not telling the whole truth?

To be continued…